MW00769169

BESSIE, BOP, OR BACH

Collected Stories

Ran Walker

COOL EMPIRE PRESS

Other Books by Ran Walker

The Race of Races: A Novel

Four Floors (with Sabin Prentis)

Afro Nerd in Love: A Novella

The Keys of My Soul: A Novel

Mojo's Guitar: A Novel/
Il etait une fois Morris Jones (Editions Autrement)

30 Love: A Novel

B-Sides and Remixes: A Novel

TABLE OF CONTENTS

The Secret of Alice Breedlove

Charlotte Stephens sat quietly, one hand interlocked with her husband's, the other flapping the nauseating heat of the church with a McWilliams Mortuary cardboard fan. The sanctuary was filled beyond its designed capacity, and a number of folding chairs had been placed in the aisles between the pews. Still, people stood along the walls, their cramped bodies attempting to stay erect in the thick and growing heat of the room. The air conditioner had malfunctioned earlier that morning, and the ushers had placed electric fans in various corners of the church, which did little more than blow the humid Oak Bluff, Mississippi, air from one side of the room to the other.

"Daddy, it's hot in here!" Rita said, tugging at her father's pant leg. Her butterscotch skin glistened with perspiration.

When Eric Stephens failed to acknowledge her comment, she reached across him and swatted Charlotte's leg. "Mama, it's hot! I'm gonna pass out!"

Charlotte shot her daughter an evil look. "Be quiet!" she whispered sharply.

Her six-year-old daughter pretended to faint from the heat, melodramatically falling against Eric's arm.

Charlotte reached behind a hymnal situated on the back of the pew in front of them and pulled out another fan. She handed the fan to Eric, and he waved it slowly back and forth between Rita and himself.

The preacher yelled and screamed in the pulpit, jumping around and exclaiming that Alice Breedlove had been a pillar of the community, that she was a mother, a grandmother, a great-grandmother, and a woman who was loved by all. With all of the generic epithets he tossed around, Charlotte wondered if he knew any real details of Grandma Alice's life, beyond her perpetual tithing.

The extended family had taken up one half of the sanctuary, with other members of the community filling in the other seats and spaces along the walls. Charlotte, Eric, and Rita were seated near the back of the church, where the only temptation had been whether or not to ease out of the exit several feet from their pew and race for the air conditioner in their car or to sit and behave like bereaved family members were supposed to behave.

"And, uh," the preacher said, clearing his throat, "we realize that today is not a sad day, but a day of joy, uh, because Sister Breedlove has gone home to be with the Lord." His large dark body, draped in an overflowing black robe, seemed to hover over the flower displays framing the closed casket.

Charlotte leaned in closer to Eric, further sandwiching Rita. She glanced at him and could tell that he was ready to go. Although she knew he loved Grandma Alice as much as she did, Charlotte knew her husband wasn't much for spectacles, and with the heat compounding everything else, Rita's melodramatic fainting could have very well been Charlotte's own.

Still the preacher raved, "We know, uh, that Sister Breedlove was not, uh, perfect. But none of us are perfect. And, uh, we know that she's looking down on us right now, er-uh, smiling and saying, 'Don't you worry 'bout me. I'm with the Lord now.'"

Charlotte felt the sting in her eyes, but she didn't know if it was perspiration or tears. She missed Grandma Alice, but there was something in the back of her mind that irked her. It tied back to Grandma Alice's last days and her refusal to answer certain questions about something that had nearly torn the family apart. Charlotte didn't know the details, but she knew that her aunts and uncles were very concerned about those answers. It was a chance for Grandma Alice to provide some peace of mind to her children. But as she lay on her hospice bed, she ignored the questions and the various ways in which those questions were pleaded, choosing to focus her eyes on the ceiling instead. Only Uncle Nathan was there when she passed away, and because she had not spoken in several days, no one was sure what her last words were or why she felt content in taking those answers that might have liberated her family to her grave.

Following the interment, the extended family gathered at Grandma Alice's house for the traditional "home-going" meal. Since a family of that magnitude rarely saw each other all at once, such occasions, whether during funerals or weddings, required a bit of socializing before returning to one's respective hometown. Grandma Alice's youngest son, Nathan, who was living in the house when Grandma Alice passed away, had been deeded the house months earlier and had now opened it to everyone who had come to town for the funeral.

Charlotte could smell the smoking charcoals coming from the barbecue grill and hear the sounds of Earth, Wind & Fire blasting from the small boom box in the front yard as she walked toward the house. Several of her cousins leaned against the side of the house sipping beers, while the smaller children ran around the yard. Rita, as if she was about to burst, joined in, racing to the red clay dunes behind the house, much to Charlotte's chagrin. Eric whispered to Charlotte that they should let her play, since she hadn't acted up too badly during the funeral, a funeral, he reminded her, that lasted nearly two hours in a church with a broken air conditioner.

Charlotte found a seat at the kitchen table with her aunts and cousins. Eric, taking his cue, eased himself into a game of spades that had been set up in the adjacent living room area.

"She seemed like she was doing so much better since the doctors released her," Aunt Sadie said.

"That's the way it always happen. Someone look like they gon' get better, and then you look up and they dead," Charlotte's older cousin Tillie responded. "Poor soul."

As Charlotte listened to the women talking about Grandma Alice, she was once again sensed there was something unanswered hanging in the air. The answer probably resided in one of the women at the table.

"Can someone tell me why Grandpa Buddy and Grandma Alice got divorced?" Charlotte asked. She didn't know why she felt compelled to ask that question, but it had been something lingering in her mind for a while. She wondered if the answer might have been tied to the answers the other family members were still seeking.

A hush came over the table, and Charlotte realized that she had touched a nerve. She was family, but even family couldn't ask certain questions and expect an answer.

Aunt Sadie broke the silence. "I was fourteen when Mama and Daddy split. All of us went with Daddy when he moved to Chicago to take that job with the school system. That was back in the fifties."

The circle of women seemed to open up after Sadie's comment. Charlotte knew that what she was going to hear was what the older family members referred to in hushed tones as "grown folks business." Although she was nearly thirty, she realized that her aunts were finally seeing her as one of them.

Aunt Amanda said, "I still remember getting in the car and watching Mama stand on the porch, waving at us. I wondered why she didn't do more to keep us. I think I cried all the way to Chicago."

Cousin Tillie shook her head in consolation. "I know that had to be hard."

"Too hard," Aunt Amanda responded.

"Why didn't Grandma Alice go with y'all to Chicago?" Charlotte asked.

"You really don't know?" Aunt Amanda said.

Charlotte shook her head.

Aunt Sadie leaned on the table, her thick dark arms resembling logs about to tumble forth. "Mama was cheating on Daddy."

Charlotte swallowed hard. This was the first time that she had heard any of this, and she wondered how she had made it this far in her life without hearing this bit of what was apparently common knowledge to everyone else.

"Did they ever find out who it was?" Cousin Tillie asked.

Aunt Sadie shook her head. "Some people say it was Ole Barry Wideman. Other folks think it was James Gunn. But there ain't no one who knows for sure."

"Then how do you know that Grandma Alice really stepped out on Granddaddy?" Charlotte asked. "Maybe all of this is just gossip from the corner store."

Aunt Amanda responded slowly, "It wasn't no gossip, not if Daddy believed it."

"There was definitely someone else," Aunt Sadie said matter-of-factly.

"How do you know for sure?" Charlotte asked.

"A woman just knows," Aunt Sadie said, daring Charlotte to challenge her.

Charlotte lowered her head, her voice almost a whisper. "Is that what you guys wanted her to tell you when she was on her deathbed?"

Aunt Sadie pounded her fists on the table, startling everyone, and stood up. "It was the least that she could have done!"

When Uncle Nathan barreled through the door with a huge pan of barbecued chicken and an enormous smile on his face, a feeling of relief spread over the room and the conversation was considered finished.

"All I'm saying is that whatever happened between your grandparents was so long ago that you shouldn't dwell on it. Before your grandfather died, he and your grandmother were still close friends. Weren't they?" Eric inquired, sitting on the edge of the full-sized hotel bed later that night.

"They were close, yes," Charlotte responded, rubbing Rita's sleeping head. The child had fallen asleep lying across her lap, and Charlotte hadn't felt like moving Rita to the other bed yet.

"Just focus on the good things you experienced with her. It's not good to open up wounds if they've already healed," Eric said. "Promise me you'll let this thing rest."

Charlotte nodded her head.

"Eric, honey," she said, lifting Rita. "Can you pull back the spread on the other bed?"

Eric pulled back the sheets and scooped up his daughter from his wife's lap, placing her gently down onto the bed. He tucked her in, softly kissing her cheek. Stretching his six-foot frame, he sat back down on the other bed next to Charlotte.

"I love you, baby."

"I love you too, Charlotte. Everything'll be all right. Let's just let your grandmother be at peace. She lived her life as best she could."

"You're right."

"And you're beautiful," he said, leaning over to kiss her while turning off the lamp between the beds.

The following morning Charlotte awoke refreshed, surprised at how well she slept.

"Good morning, handsome," she said brightly, leaning over and kissing Eric.

"Umm," he said struggling to open his eyes. "Someone must have had a good night's sleep."

Charlotte smiled.

She sat up in the bed and glanced over at Rita. For a moment she contemplated sneaking in an amorous episode with Eric, but quickly thought against it when Rita started to twist and turn in her sleep.

"I'm going to go ahead and get my shower," Eric said, rising to his feet.

"Okay," Charlotte said. "Are we still planning on stopping by Grandma Alice's house before we head back to Daily?"

"Sure. That sounds good. Plus I wanted to get a copy of this album Nathan let me listen to yesterday."

Eric grabbed his bathrobe and walked into the bathroom. Charlotte went over to the other bed and sat down next to Rita. She considered waking her, but decided against it when she saw that it was only eight o'clock in the morning. Instead, she pulled out Rita's clothes for the day and put up the ironing board.

By ten o'clock, the Stephens family was pulling into the gravel driveway of Grandma Alice's house. Uncle Nathan was up and wide-awake, entertaining the few relatives who had decided to spend the night. The scent of buttermilk biscuits, sausage, and scrambled eggs filled the small three-room house, and Charlotte found her mouth watering as soon as she passed through the front door.

"Go ahead and fix yourself a plate," Uncle Nathan said.

Charlotte and Eric sat down next to Nathan and the other family members, while Rita took her plate in front of the television set in the den.

"How are you holding up, Uncle Nathan?" Charlotte asked between bites.

"You know, it still ain't sunk in yet. I guess when all of the company leaves it'll really hit me."

Eric placed his hand on Uncle Nathan's shoulder. "If you need anything, don't hesitate to call us."

"I appreciate that," Uncle Nathan said. He lowered his head solemnly and continued nibbling at the food on his plate. "Hey, Charlotte, feel free to go back in Mama's old room and pick up anything you want. One of her last wishes was for the women in the family to just pick what they wanted from the personal belongings in her bedroom. I have to warn you though that Tillie and Amanda done already raided a lot of the good stuff."

"That's fine," Charlotte responded. She couldn't imagine anything that she would want out of Grandma Alice's closet, but she felt that she should at least take something she could give to Rita one day as an heirloom.

After she finished her breakfast, Charlotte slipped away to Grandma Alice's bedroom down the hall. The room looked as if it hadn't been lived in for several months. Surprisingly, it was immaculate, considering people had already rummaged through a number of personal items. The dresser that normally bore Grandma Alice's small jewelry box was no longer there, nor was the jewelry box. Most of the church hats were gone. The pictures on the dresser had all been removed. In fact, there wasn't much in the room that Charlotte felt she *could* take.

Turning around, she secretly hoped that the closet hadn't been raided like the rest of the room had. She pulled back the doors to the closet and ran her hand along a series of dresses and suits still on the hangers. Grandma Alice was a size 24, and Charlotte was a size 10, so there wasn't much need in focusing on clothing. Charlotte reached up and ran her hands along the top shelf of the closet. There were a few of Grandma Alice's more exotic church hats. Staring at the closet, Charlotte didn't see anything that she would want to take with her. Her greedy cousins and aunts had already taken the obvious things, like jewelry and pictures.

Charlotte looked down at the shoes strewn about the closet floor. The mess the others left would have upset Grandma Alice. It was a good thing that the only real property Grandma Alice had owned had been transferred by deed to Nathan several months before she died, or the family might have wound up fighting over that, too. Charlotte lowered herself onto her knees and began organizing the random shoes into neat pairs across the foot of the closet. Some of the shoes looked as if they had never been worn; others looked as though they had seen much better days.

As Charlotte picked up a pair of red pumps (what was Grandma Alice doing with those?) and placed them in the back of the closet, she noticed that the carpet back there had been cut. With the shoes thrown about haphazardly, the cuts were nearly invisible. Charlotte peeled back the strip of carpet to find a wooden floorboard cut in a rectangular fashion. There was a small hole on the back left corner of the board, just large enough to hook a pinky finger through it and pull the board up. Charlotte lifted it and found that a small hole had been cut into the floor, just large enough to hold the shoebox situated inside.

She carefully retrieved the box from the compartment in the floor. She was curious as to what Grandma Alice might have been hiding. How long had the box been there? Charlotte looked around the closet and found a few pairs of shoes still in their boxes. She grabbed a few of them and stacked them on top of the other box, hoping to disguise what she had discovered. She set the stack of boxes off to the side and ran her hand around in the hole just to make sure she wasn't missing anything. The space was empty, so she returned the floorboard to its place and situated the carpet, moving some of the shoes randomly across the floor to cover the spot.

Still kneeling in the closet, Charlotte placed the top shoeboxes to the side and lifted the lid on the one she had unearthed from the floorboard. She was speechless when she discovered the box was filled with letters—no jewelry or money, only worn envelopes.

"Mommy?" Rita was walking down the hall toward Grandma Alice's room.

Charlotte quickly placed the lid on top of the box, stacking the other boxes on top. "Yes, Rita. In here."

"Hey, Mommy," Rita said, walking into the room. "What are you doing?"

Charlotte stood with boxes in her hands. "I'm just getting a few things to remember your great-grandmother by, baby."

"Ooh, can I see?"

"I'll show you when we get home. Okay?"

"Okay," Rita responded, as Charlotte escorted her from the room.

"You guys be safe headed back," Uncle Nathan said, patting the roof of the car.

"Thanks. And remember what I said: If you need anything, just call," Eric said.

"Hey, Charlotte," Uncle Nathan said. "Find everything all right in Mama's room?"

"Just fine. I picked up a few boxes of shoes."

"Good. Whatever is left over I'll probably just give away to the church. See you guys next time."

Uncle Nathan stood back from the car and waved as it pulled out of the driveway and headed off down the narrow country road back to Daily.

Charlotte could barely wait to reopen the box the following morning after Eric left for work. Since he had opened his own orthodontics practice, he had pressured her into leaving her dead-end job as a deputy clerk at the circuit clerk's office. Now she was what one of her former co-workers referred to as a "domestic engineer." Her job description now included getting up in the morning and getting everyone ready: Rita for first grade over at Tuck Elementary School and Eric at Stephens Orthodontics. Throughout the day, she would run errands, maintain the rather large house (three levels, including a basement), and work on a weekly advice column she had managed to get in a small, local black newspaper.

As she sat down on the floor of her bedroom, she removed the lid from the shoebox and emptied the envelopes onto the carpet. The handwriting on them was identical. They were all from a "P. L. Cole" in Bartlett, Tennessee. The postmarks, however, went back to July of 1955. There seemed to be at least one or two letters from each year leading up to two years ago. Charlotte didn't realize that there had been that many letters in the box. Although the shoebox was large, it never occurred to her that it could hold so much paper.

Quickly she shifted the letters into stacks according to the dates. She doubted that she could read all of the letters in a single day, but she vowed to start. The curiosity of knowing why Grandma Alice had kept up with these letters was overwhelming. Who was P. L. Cole? How could Grandma Alice have been corresponding with this person for all these years without anyone knowing? Why were these letters hidden away in the back of her closet?

Charlotte lifted the first envelope. It was a single page written in neat, legible cursive.

My Dearest Alice,
I hope this letter finds you doing much better. I am very sorry to hear about your divorce, although it brings a relief to my aching heart. I know that all of this must be very painful for you,

*especially since he took the children with him. I have resorted to
writing you because I feel as if my phone calls were what lead to
the current situation. I am truly sorry. I just could not resist the
urge to hear your voice again, to dance beneath its melody and lose
myself in your words. For any pain I have caused you, I
apologize. I just wanted you to know that I love you very much,
and I miss the moments we shared in each other's arms. I don't
believe I will ever find anyone else who could bring out this feeling
in me, and I find myself yearning to be with you again, kiss you,
and dissolve into you. Should you want to reach me, I am now
living right outside of Memphis, Tennessee, at the address above.*
    With all of my heart,
    P. L.

"Oh, my God!" Charlotte said, shaking her head in
disbelief. She reread the letter, unable to put it down.

From looking at the other letters, it became clear
that there had been a correspondence going on between
Grandma Alice and this man for some time. Hit with
the sudden knowledge of the affair, she quickly rose to
her feet and began pacing the bedroom. Did she really
want to go any deeper than where she had already been?
She knew that she couldn't bring herself to tell anyone
what she'd found out until she knew the whole story,
and as she looked down, it appeared the whole story
had been laid out in writing before her feet.

Charlotte read on until it was time to pick up Rita
from school. Before leaving the house, she sectioned

off the letters that she read from the ones she had yet to read and sealed them in the box, tucking them away in her closet. She smiled when she realized she was hiding the letters (which she had found hidden in another closet) in her own closet.

For the rest of the afternoon, while she began to prepare for dinner, her mind was stuck on her discovery. In the subsequent letters, it was clear that Grandma Alice had confessed her love in return for this P. L. Cole because the letters had become even more amorous. Still the letters were coming twice or maybe three times a year, which suggested that Grandma Alice might have been talking to P. L. on the phone or traveling to visit him in between letters.

P. L. was definitely a Southern name if Charlotte had ever heard one. Back in her grandmother's days, it was not uncommon for men to have names that were merely initials. In fact, she had two uncles once removed with initials for names. She didn't know if that was because the midwives couldn't spell out the full names or not. It was just something that people accepted. In Charlotte's mind, having a name of initials still beat the idea of being named Junior, a name often given to people in that area who were not named after anyone at all.

Charlotte finished all of the letters that afternoon, and with nervousness building inside of her like a small flame inching closer to gasoline, she was already beginning to plan her next step.

Sitting down to dinner, Eric asked if anything exciting had happened that day.

The question rattled Charlotte, and she quickly found herself lying to her husband. "Nothing much. Just worked a little on my column and took care of few errands."

She couldn't bring herself to tell him that she had been going through her grandmother's old love letters, the proof that Grandma Alice had been an adulteress. She knew that he wouldn't understand why she had to know about her grandmother's private life. He had already expressed his adamant desire for her to stop snooping around in her grandmother's life. What would he say if she told him that her snooping had uncovered one of the greatest secrets of the Breedlove family? Knowing her husband, she figured he wouldn't be particularly pleased, so she decided it was something he didn't have to know about.

"What about you, Rita? How was school today?" Eric continued.

"Okay."

"Just okay?"

"Well, this boy in my class, Timmy, called me a dufus at lunch. I hit him on his arm."

Eric looked at Rita, attempting to conceal his smile. "You know when boys your age pick on girls, that usually means that they like them."

"Yuck! He's so gross. Ewww, Daddy!"

Eric and Charlotte laughed. The laughter came as a huge relief to Charlotte as she allowed it to shake her body.

"Baby," Eric said leaning toward Charlotte. "You know I have to go out of town tomorrow to that dental conference in Jackson. The session lets out at four-thirty, so I expect to get back here around seven tomorrow evening."

She had forgotten about the conference. Eric was on a panel to speak on some of the updates in the field of orthodontics. She was somewhat embarrassed that she had forgotten something so important to him.

"Do you have everything together?"

"I think I have everything. I put together some handouts of my PowerPoint presentation and had them copied this afternoon. It should go well."

"I'll lay out your suit before we go to bed."

"Thanks, baby," Eric said, as he rose to wipe down the table and put the dishes in the sink.

By the time Charlotte crawled into bed next to Eric, she knew what she had to do: she had to go to Bartlett, Tennessee, and find out everything she could about P. L. Cole from the man himself. It was only a two-hour drive. If she left out around the same time that Eric left for work she would make it back in plenty of time as to not rouse suspicion. But then there was Rita to consider.

She nudged Eric, who had just slipped off to sleep. He shifted and turned toward her.

"Hmff," he exhaled, not quite awake.

She shook him until he sat up in the bed. "Yes, baby," he finally said.

"I want to run some errands tomorrow, and it'll probably take up the majority of the day. Do you mind if we let Rita catch the school bus to Mrs. Thomas's?"

Mrs. Earline Thomas, a sweet widow not yet sixty, was the designated babysitter whenever Eric and Charlotte wanted to get away for a weekend. For the first three years of Rita's life, she spent much of her time in the safe, comfortable confines of Mrs. Thomas's small house on Den Street. When Charlotte let go of her job at the courthouse, there wasn't much need for Mrs. Thomas's services. Now, however, Mrs. Thomas seemed like a godsend. Charlotte waited anxiously for Eric's response.

"Sure, baby. I just need to get some rest before I get on the road in the morning."

"Thanks," she said kissing him lightly. She snuggled under him as she began to plan her trip.

Charlotte could finally exhale after Eric and Rita left the house. That morning Eric had asked her what she needed to do that day. She concocted a story about needing to pick up some supplies for her home office and follow up on some query letters for magazines she had been trying to crack for the last six months.

After she showered, she went online to see if P. L. Cole's address was the same one that she had scribbled down off of the envelopes. As she looked at the Yellow Pages online, she was tempted to call Mr. Cole first. She quickly dismissed the idea though. For what she wanted to know, she felt she'd have a better chance of getting the information if she were to show up in person unexpectedly. In large part her plan relied on some degree of surprise.

Charlotte grabbed the shoebox of letters and got into her SUV, headed towards Bartlett.

As she pulled into Mr. Cole's driveway, it began to dawn on her that maybe this was not the smartest idea she had ever had. She had driven the two hours to get to Bartlett without letting her husband know what she was up to. Was she crazy? What if her car broke down? How would she explain this? Her nerves overcoming her, she started backing out of the driveway when she saw someone walk past the window. Maybe that's P. L. Cole, she thought as she pulled her vehicle back into the driveway. She turned the motor off and sat with the shoebox on her lap as she contemplated what to do. If she knocked on the door, she would probably come to find out about her grandmother's secret life; if she stayed in her vehicle, she could have gone on living her life in a blissful ignorance to the depth of what she had already discovered. She opened the door to the truck and stepped out. No turning back now, she told herself as she walked up the old worn steps of the small wooden house.

She pressed the doorbell, her nerves jittery, the shoebox resting by her side. She could hear a pair of feet shuffling slowly toward the door from the other side.

"Yes," a soft crackling voice responded. "What do you want?"

Although there was a peephole in the door, whoever was standing on the other side was not about to open the door until it made sense to do so.

"My name is Charlotte Stephens, and I'm looking for Mr. P. L. Cole," Charlotte stammered.

"Who are you?"

"I just wanted to meet him. I believe he knew my grandmother, Alice Breedlove."

Slowly the door cracked open. A weathered, old hand reached around to unlock the screen door and push it open. "Come in."

Charlotte walked into the house, her nerves still knotting into a ball in her stomach. Her legs were weighted as she stepped across the threshold into the foyer. The house was very neat, but it had a feeling of being really old. The door closed behind her, and she saw an elderly woman with a deep mocha complexion standing there, locking the door back.

"Oh," Charlotte said. Apparently the raspy voice she had heard was this woman's. She quickly became afraid that she might have said too much. Her objective was never to come to the house and cause marital friction between Mr. Cole and his wife. Immediately she began to fear that she had caused irreparable damage. "I'm sorry. Are you Mrs. Cole?"

The old woman smiled. "Come in," she said, guiding Charlotte into the living room. "Have a seat. Would you like some tea?"

"No thank you," Charlotte said. She was beginning to feel very uncomfortable about the situation, but she couldn't tell why.

"So you're here to see P. L. Cole?" the woman asked carefully. "And you're Alice Breedlove's granddaughter?"

"Yes, ma'am," Charlotte said, remembering how much information she had revealed outside the door.

The woman paused for a moment. "Does anyone know you're here asking around?"

The question was a peculiar one. In the silence that followed, something dawned on Charlotte. She had made one very obvious assumption about P. L. Cole, and she was just coming to understand how incorrect her assumption had been.

"Are you P. L. Cole?" Charlotte asked, her heart beating rapidly. She could sense the response even before it escaped the old woman's lips.

The old woman stared at Charlotte for a moment, through her gray eyes, as if considering how she should proceed. Finally, her head lowered and rose in repetition. "Pearlie Lynette Cole."

For a moment all Charlotte could do was stare at the old woman. It was as if everything had come to a halt and she was suspended in time gazing upon the face of the woman who had been her grandmother's lover for over five decades. Her head filled with a million questions, but she wasn't sure that she needed any answers—at least that's what a part of her wanted to believe. It would have been easy to just walk away from the situation, but her feet would not move, nor would her curiosity budge.

Charlotte examined Ms. Cole's face, hoping to see what her grandmother had seen in this woman all those years ago. Ms. Cole's face was unremarkable beneath her aging exterior. The woman had to have been roughly eighty years old. Her slight frame helped to underscore just how different her build was from Grandma Alice's. In many ways they were simply opposites: Grandma Alice had been a larger, more attractive woman with a lighter complexion, whereas Ms. Cole was a darker, thin, plain-looking woman. Yet this woman had captured Grandma Alice's heart.

Charlotte placed the shoebox on her lap and opened it. "You wrote these letters?" she asked, handing one over to Ms. Cole.

"Oh my," Ms. Cole sighed, examining the frail piece of paper. She stared at it and looked up at the box full of other letters. "I can't believe she kept all of those."

"Yes. She had them hidden away in the floorboard of her closet. I came across them accidentally." Charlotte paused. "How did you get to know my grandmother?"

Ms. Cole sat back in her chair and crossed her thin arms. She was silent for so long that Charlotte had assumed she had no plans to say anything further. If that was the case, Charlotte would understand. When Ms. Cole finally opened her mouth and spoke, Charlotte was both surprised and relieved.

"I never thought I'd ever have to tell anyone any of this. I thought that all of this would be a secret between Alice and me that we would take to our graves."

"Why take it to your graves? There are a lot of same sex couples out there."

"Charlotte, is it? Your grandmother and I, we came up in a different time. I met her right around the close of World War II, when your grandfather was away in Europe serving as a chaplain. I was working at a local laundry house when Alice started working there. My husband was killed in the war a year and a half earlier, and—I don't know. We just became friends. We were friends for a while and things just kind of went from there. It was like she filled something in me that was empty, and I tried to do the same for her."

Charlotte liked the old woman's voice. She spoke with a soothing confidence, her diction quite the opposite of Grandma Alice's. Ms. Cole, for all of her understated appearance, had a manner about her that suggested that not only was she smart, but she was cultured.

Charlotte wanted to ask who had made the first move. She couldn't imagine her grandmother making a pass at a widow, but she realized that she couldn't imagine a widow making a pass at Grandma Alice either. All of it was difficult for her to wrap her mind around.

"Alice was a very special woman. After the divorce, it took her several months before she would even communicate with me. I think she felt guilty about everything. I know I did. I mean, here I was a widow doing something that I had been raised to believe was wrong. Before Alice, I had never had a real interest in women, although I suspect it was there all along.

"She was really something special. She used to have this summer hat that she would wear, and her long Choctaw hair, that's what she used to call it, hanging down her shoulders. She looked like a queen going for a stroll through the palace grounds." Ms. Cole smiled, her lips revealing her large false teeth.

As Charlotte sat listening to Ms. Cole reminisce about the relationship she had had with Grandma Alice, Charlotte realized something: whatever they had was much stronger than what Grandma Alice and Grandpa Buddy had had. And as Charlotte considered that thought, it slowly dawned on her that Grandpa Buddy had probably realized the same thing. He had to have known how Grandma Alice felt. That's why he left quietly and never revealed the secret to anyone.

Charlotte listened attentively as Ms. Cole told her how the relationship had quietly dissipated when Grandpa Buddy became ill, which coincided with the last letters Ms. Cole had sent Grandma Alice. During Grandpa Buddy's last months, Grandma Alice had undertaken the responsibility of caring for him, although she had not been his wife for more than forty years. That's when the relationship ended, Charlotte thought. As she pondered this, she felt a pity for Ms. Cole, who had apparently been placed on the backburner while Grandma Alice went about the job of easing the discomfort of Grandpa Buddy's final days.

"I miss Alice. I was devastated when I read about her passing in the Daily Tribune. You know, I had subscribed to that paper after I didn't hear back from her. There was no other way for me to know what was going on there." She paused. "Sometimes I'm sad because she's gone. Other times I'm angry that she cut me off, but I guess I understand. I'm old enough to know that you have to just be thankful for the time that you had with someone, and I'm thankful that Alice allowed me to know real love during my lifetime," Ms. Cole said.

Charlotte rose to her feet. "Here," she said, handing Ms. Cole the shoebox full of letters. "I'm sure Grandma Alice would have wanted you to have these or she would not have kept them."

"Thank you," Ms. Cole said. Her eyes moistened as she took the box in her delicate hands.

Charlotte left Bartlett early enough to beat Eric home. As she drove, her mind raced through the events of the past few days. She had discovered Grandma Alice's secret, a secret that two people had already taken to their graves.   She thought about Ms. Cole's tear-stained cheeks as she had hugged the old woman goodbye. There were now only two people who held the secret, and Charlotte had decided that, like Pearlie Lynette Cole, she was content in taking that secret to her grave, too.

A Night With Nina Simone

The letter arrived several hours before the storm set in. It was mixed in with undesirable mail and would have remained in a loose stack of envelopes and coupons at the edge of my dining room table, had I not caught a glimpse of the penmanship.

She had been gone a month and had taken back everything she had managed to conveniently leave in my one-bedroom apartment over the last three years. One of my closets had been devoted to her clothes, not to mention her shoes had cluttered the floors of all of the other closets in the apartment. Even the electric toothbrush that had sat next to my dogged Oral-B was gone. She had left while I was taping my show over at the radio station, and when I finally made it home, only a short handwritten note and my spare key were lying on the table waiting for me. The rest of the apartment was empty, save the few belongings she left scattered about the small space.

I had read over her Dear John letter so many times I had memorized it. I never paid enough attention to her, it said. I was holding her back from her true potential. But the best part of all was an evasive allusion to her having found someone with whom she shared a better "connection." After going through the textbook arc of emotions, I was content to never hear from her again. But then the letter came.

I stared at it with contempt, as if our silent treaty had been broken.

Something in my stomach fluttered. I sat down, unsure of whether to open the letter or warm up the leftover Chinese food in the back of my refrigerator.

I opted for the Chinese food.

Swirling the greasy lo mein around my fork and pouring the mysterious, pungent sauce over what I believed to be chicken, I gradually found that I could not look away from the letter. My mind became filled with curiosity, and without realizing it, I scanned through the various possibilities of its contents. Maybe she wanted to see if we could rebuild our friendship, or maybe she wanted to admit that her actions had been hasty and that she really wanted to come home. I didn't know whether or not the latter was wishful thinking or an honest assumption, but after I took several more bites, I picked up the envelope and jaggedly opened it with my index finger.

The letter, like the softness of a boiled egg beneath a cracked shell, rested on the table unharmed by my careless ripping of the envelope, and for some reason I

handled the actual letter with a sort of gentleness, as if
her words had a fragile body of their own and I had a
duty to protect them. I moved my food out of the way
and carefully unfolded the letter, which appeared to be a
single page, across the placemat in front of me.
Expecting to see a flurry of words, I was surprised to
see only a few sentences:

Dear Jasper,

*I hope this letter finds you in good spirits. I am doing very
well on this end. I recently discovered that I left a few of my
belongings at your apartment. In particular, I left my Nina
Simone CDs over there. Please feel free to mail them to me when
you get a free moment. You can use the address on this envelope.*

Thanks, Melissa

The letter was direct and unembellished, but I
couldn't help scrutinizing it, holding it up to the light to
gaze between the lines for any deeper resonance from
the words. After reading through the letter twice, I
knew that her concern for my wellbeing was secondary
to the CD collection she had accidentally left.

I tossed the letter onto the table, frustrated. I hated
to acknowledge that I still cared about her, and I guess I
subconsciously wanted the letter to reflect some
requited feelings. Instead, I got a short, detached
message requesting a stack of CDs that I didn't even
realize were still in the apartment.

The letter angered me, and for a moment, all I could
think about was telling her where she could get off.

Then it dawned on me that I didn't have a phone number, e-mail address, or any other way of contacting her, with the exception of the post office box address on the letter I had received. If I wanted to play her game, I would have to play by her rules.

I laid the letter back on the table and attempted to eat a few more bites of the cooling lo mein before finally giving up and dumping the remains in a plastic bag, tying it, and tossing it in the trashcan. I wanted to ignore the letter, but the whole act of reading it had brought back a stream of happy memories about Melissa and me. I could hear the sound of her high-pitched laughter and see that dimple in her right cheek dancing. I could smell the light scent of her perfume and feel the tickle of her soft hair on my nose. I could see those funky glasses of hers resting on the bridge of her nose, like a hip librarian. Even the feel of her kiss moving across my face before resting on my lips left me unable to move. She was the woman my family adored and the woman my boys had adopted as a member of the crew. But more than anything, I loved her, and that love made me want to be a better man. I was pre-programmed to interpret her leaving as an indictment of my inadequacy. As a result, when she left, I knew I wasn't good enough for her—even at my best.

I wrestled with my memories a bit longer, before deciding to take a glance around the apartment, in its various nooks and crannies, to see if I could, in fact, find the CDs. I looked around the den and dining room areas, and after having no success, I entered the bedroom. For nearly an hour, I combed through drawers, looked up under the bed and mattresses, and ran my hand across nearly every corner of the closet. When I finally got tired enough to sit on my bed, the thought settled over me that now I must be an even bigger fool than I had been when she left me. Here I was tearing through my apartment looking for a stack of CDs like I was a dog hell-bent on playing fetch with a sadistic master. I walked over to the door and clicked off the light.

No sooner than I turned off the light, thunder crashed loudly outside the window. I hated thunderstorms, their unpredictable sounds and flashes. Many nights, Melissa and I would snuggle beneath the heavy comforter on my bed, intertwined in anxious ecstasy, in an effort to ignore the tumult outside. But now I could feel the storm coming down around me, and I could hear the booming sound resonating in the empty space.

I walked briskly through the apartment turning off appliances I thought could be affected by the lightning. Within moments, the only thing illuminating my apartment was the glowing light of the candles Melissa, thankfully, did not take with her when she left.

With my house smelling like wild raspberries and Chinese food, I walked into the bathroom, holding the candle as though it were an awkward substitute for a flashlight. As I carefully positioned myself in front of the toilet, the flame, now resting on the sink, rippled across a box-like formation on the floor behind the magazine rack.   Once I flushed, I knelt down and picked up what turned out to be a stack of CDs. I held them near the light and fanned through them. Each and every one of them was a Nina Simone album. "Why didn't she just get a greatest hits or something?" I muttered aloud, for no reason other than to express my frustration with having found the thing that would close down my tie to Melissa. I had never listened to a single song before, yet she felt so strongly about this stack of plastic that she wrote a letter, officially ending her silence. She hadn't requested the candles, just the CDs.

I stared at the artwork on the covers, examining the deep rich hue of the woman's skin, her nose, her lips, the various styles of her hair, and those eyes—those unfazed eyes—that had seen things that I imagine few people had ever seen. Nina could have been Melissa's mother, so closely did the two women resemble each other. Now I could see why Melissa would sometimes wear her hair in a stylish beehive wrap.

I took the CDs back into my room.   The overwhelming need to hear the music caused me to momentarily forget the storm brewing outside.   I quickly plugged in the stereo and placed one of the CDs into the unit.

"I put a spell on you--because you're mine," Nina sang. Her voice was heavy and intoxicating, like a cognac swirling restlessly around an empty belly. For a moment, I imagined a woman standing in the back of an old church house nestled in the woods off of some gravel road, her voice like warm molasses blanketing the starving souls of the congregation. I had never heard a voice like that, and I instantly felt a shiver trickle down my back.

The piano and strings sauntered behind her voice as she went into scatting incantations that were almost tangible in the stillness of the room. Through her words, I could see my relationship replaying itself, except this time things looked different.

"I love you! I love you! I love you anyhow, and I don't care if you don't want me. I'm yours right now!" Nina continued to sing.

Had I really taken Melissa for granted? Had I really neglected to show her the kind of love she deserved? Maybe I had and didn't know it.

Now I could feel Melissa's pain along side my own, and sadness wrapped itself around my face like a mask, my eyes weakening beneath its weight. I lifted my face and felt the cooling droplets descend, as if they had been transported magically from outside of my window.

Looking out into the storming night sky, I could hear the thunder's clap echoing rhythmically in the distance, and in the glow of the wild raspberry candle that kissed the darkness of my room, Nina's voice entered me, like a spirit.

I wrestled with it, wanting to reject its truth.

I had to.

But I couldn't.

Melissa was gone, and there was nothing I could do about that anymore, other than send her those CDs—

something I had already decided, even as the storm calmed around me, that I would never do.

Miss Anne's Cure for the Broken-Hearted

The sign in Miss Anne's window said that she could cure heartache for fifty dollars. In my gut I doubted it—and fifty dollars was hardly small change for me— but I had reached a place in my mind where I would have paid Miss Anne a thousand dollars if she could erase the memories of Tonya Stewart from my head.

If I had better reigns on my heart, I would have been three years, four months, and two days beyond the dull ache that clouded my chest like the suck of muddy red clay. I had made progress in going cold turkey, and things might've continued on that way, had I not seen the wedding announcement on page six of *The Daily Chronicle*. As I stared at the picture of the two of them, I couldn't stop myself from wondering who the hell that guy was and how had he gotten Tonya to do something that I couldn't do in five years: say "yes."

Miss Anne's sign might've been something that I would've taken a picture of with my cell phone, only to laugh at later with friends, but that day, for some indescribable reason, it felt like this elderly woman might—just might—have been able to cure me once and for all.

The store looked even smaller on the inside than it had on the outside. A small circular table sat in the center of the room with two chairs, one on either side. The drab brown walls and funky orange and green beaded curtains gave the space a rustic seventies feel. The chimes on the front door continued jingling as it closed slowly behind me.

"One moment," Miss Anne called out from the back of the store, in the space behind the wall that divided her personal space from the room in which I stood.

Waiting there, just a few feet inside of the store, my stomach twisted, my nerves starting to get the better of me. I could still hear my mother's voice telling me to stay away from Miss Anne, because, in her words, "the elevator didn't go all the way to the top floor." But my mother had been dead for ten years, and well, Miss Anne, who was old when I was a kid, was still around. If someone had told me that Miss Anne was over a hundred-years-old, I wouldn't have flinched. Maybe it was that longevity that made me believe that she really did have the cure for heartache—because without it, she would have surely been dust by now.

"Eric Rodman," she said, nodding to the chair across the table from hers.

Although I had never spoken to her before, my name rolled off of her tongue as if she had known it for quite some time.

"Miss Anne," I said, addressing her as respectfully as I could, "I saw your sign in the window—the one about curing heartache."

"You have a broken heart," she said matter-of-factly.

I nodded.

"How long ago did y'all break it off?"

I had assumed that Miss Anne was psychic or at least had some kind of sixth sense. If she did, she would have already known the answer to her question—the same way that she knew my name when I sat down. The fact that she was asking me questions about such basic things put me off-kilter. What could she really do for me if she wasn't psychic? But then, one didn't technically have to be psychic to provide a remedy to a problem.

I leaned forward slightly. "It's been a little over three years since we broke up, but we had been together a long time before that."

As she listened, she scrunched up her mouth, twisting her lips from side to side as if she might spit a mouthful of snuff juice onto the table. She looked so deeply into my eyes I thought she could see the back of my skull. When she finally opened her mouth, she said, "You got fiddy?"

I reached into my pocket and pulled out two twenties and a ten from my bill clip. I pushed the money across the table toward her, but she never took her eyes off of me.

"You got it bad, don't you?" she said, her voice so raspy that I expected it to break into a lung-rattling cough. "Don't worry. You ain't gotta say nothin. It's written all over your face. But you ain't the only one this month that's done come up in here lookin for the remedy."

Miss Anne suddenly rose from the table, grabbing the cash and tucking it around her large bosom into what had to have been one of the largest bras I had ever seen.

When she turned to walk away, I immediately stood. "Where are you going?"

"Cool your heels and sit down," she said. "I gotta go and get the remedy out of the back room.

I continued standing for a moment, only because I didn't want to feel like a child being told what to do, but she already had my money, so there was no real point in my posturing. I sat back down.

I could hear her ruffling around in the back, and I began to wonder exactly what her remedy for heartache would involve. Was it some type of drink, one concocted from the strangest and most random of ingredients? The thought of her waving a magical root around in a cup of orange juice made my stomach turn. Would she use eye of newt? Oh god! I didn't even know what that was. Maybe that was something that only witches used, and Miss Anne wasn't a witch, was she? Hell if I knew. All I knew for sure was if she was making some kind of drink, it would probably be the most expensive swig of something that I had paid for in some time.

Then again, maybe it was some type of powder, something that I would have to sprinkle on a particular thing in some special way. I considered if I might have to take such a powder and sprinkle it across the threshold of the church in which Tonya was to exchange her nuptials. What if the powder turned out to be something that I would have to sprinkle on her directly? We hadn't talked in a while, but if my back was against the wall, I knew I could come up with a plausible situation that would allow me to dust the hell out of her with the magic powder, if necessary.

Sitting at Miss Anne's table, my mind became restless with thoughts of how I would be able to get Tonya back. This remedy had to work. And more importantly, I had convinced myself that it would work.

When the plump, elderly woman returned with a small piece of paper dangling from her fingertips, I didn't know what to think.

She sat down across from me, placing the small sheet squarely in front of me. My eyes scanned the page looking for a recipe or something I could understand. Instead, the sheet contained only four numbers: 6611.

"What is this?" I asked immediately.

"These the numbers that's gon heal yo heart."

"With all due respect, Miss Anne, I know I didn't just pay fifty dollars for four numbers."

"I done thought about yo situation, and I believe these fo numbers is the answer."

"What are they? The numbers I should be playing in the lottery? Are they the PIN for a bank account with millions in it? Fifty dollars is a lot to pay for four numbers," I said, unable to conceal my growing exasperation.

"Now, I dun already told you that them numbers is special. But I can't be the one to tell you why. You gotta find that out fo yo self."

"So I just walk out into this town with four numbers and the meaning will be revealed to me?"

"That's right."

"How long will it take?"

"Boy, I don't have all the answers. I just know that you supposed to have them numbers and them numbers gon heal yo heartache."

I might have been a few decades younger than Miss Anne, but I wasn't a fool. I knew this woman was just running a con on me. I had given up that fifty dollars so quickly that I might as well have written it off as a donation to the Society of Life's Lessons for Beginners. I started to get up from the table and challenge the old woman, but when I glanced into her eyes, I could tell that she meant everything she had said. It was in that single moment that I realized that I had probably just given away my money to a woman whose elevator didn't quite go all the way to the top floor. In a sense, I felt sorry for her. I wasn't being conned, at least not intentionally, after all. I was merely helping an elderly woman make her rent payments. There was a part of me that couldn't feel too badly about that. She was just working the one hustle she had.

I reluctantly reached over and picked up the piece of paper, although it didn't take much of a memory to hold those four digits in my head. "Thank you," I offered weakly. "I guess I'll just go out here and make it happen then."

She smiled and nodded. "You go do that."

As I stepped back out onto the sidewalk that ran in front of the store, the bittersweet pang of the last few minutes clung in the air around me. The very streets I had walked up and down my entire life, the same streets that once saw me with Tonya in those glorious days of old, were now witnessing my breaking down into a man desperate enough to think that he could spend money to bypass the natural pain of heartache.

I had simply lost this particular battle. Tonya and I would never be together again. I knew that she would marry this guy without hesitation, and that I would just have to accept that and move on. There were greater tragedies in the world, right? I mean, I couldn't lament the inevitable when there were people in the world facing greater atrocities than a broken heart. There would be no sympathy for my little feelings, so I didn't need to play the one-man pity party. Just get on with your life, I told myself. Free advice.

On the day of the wedding, I figured that I would busy my thoughts by reorganizing my personal library. Since I had moved into my apartment several months ago, I had been stacking crates of books against the wall of the spare bedroom. Although I had been out of college for more than five years, I was still living in a place that looked like it could have been inhabited by a college frat boy. Not only was I using crates for my bookcases, I was also using several crates to hold up my 22 inch television and DVD player, as well as house the various magazine subscriptions that I still held. My primary furniture was a large futon that folded down into a queen-size bed.

As I thought briefly about Tonya's new life, I realized that it was probably time for me to get my own shit together, grow up a little more, make this space into a grown man's domicile and not just a glorified man-cave. The library in the spare room down the hall from my master bedroom was as good a place as any to start.

Half an hour later, I found myself standing in the aisle of Wal-Mart looking at some inexpensive black particle wood bookcases. I loaded several into my cart and took my time pushing the cart through the store. I didn't have a list made out before I came in, and since Wal-Mart seemed to carry everything in one place, from fresh fruit to tires, I figured taking a slow stroll through the store would help me to figure out if there was anything else I might need to pick up.

I gradually found my way to the magazine rack near the front of the store and was picking up a copy of *GQ* when I heard a soft voice call my name.

"Eric? Is that you?"

I turned toward the voice. Her face was familiar, but it was one that I had not seen in years. I fanned through my head for her name, but it was as bad as trying to work a crossword puzzle in the dark.

"Hey," I finally said.

"You don't remember my name, do you?" she asked.

Her face was beautiful beneath the harsh lights of the store, and I strained desperately to remember anything other than the fact that we went to school with each other umpteen years ago. She might have been cute then, but she was a woman who had more than come into her own by now.

"I'm trying. Help me out, please. It's been a while."

"Nancy. Nancy Clinton. I had classes with you in the tenth and eleventh grades, but then my family moved away from here before senior year."

Nancy Clinton. *Now* I could remember her. She was quiet and had always kept to herself, but she had the kind of smile that reminded you of times when life was simpler, easier.

"I remember you!" I said, trying to blow off the awkwardness of earlier. "So are you back in Daily now?"

"For a little while," she responded. "My grandmother's health is slowing down, and since my parents are still stationed in Germany, I agreed to come here and see about her."

"Oh, okay. I hope she's doing all right."

"She is. Feisty as ever. We keep telling her to slow down, but I don't think she has it in her to do that."

I nodded. "So how long have you been here? I mean, I haven't seen you around town or anything."

"It's only been a few weeks. I'm still moving things down here. I'm supposed to start up with the school system in the fall."

"You're a teacher? Cool."

"What about you?"

"I'm a paralegal for Grady Sails's firm downtown."

"Nice."

The longer I stood looking into her eyes, the more I wanted our conversation to not end.

"So how have you been spending your free time around here?" I asked.

"Just helping my grandmother out around the house. I read a lot, too. I see you have a lot of bookshelves there."

"Yeah. I'm a big reader, too. I figured it was about time that I got my collection organized."

"I'm so jealous. Most of my books are still in storage in Memphis."

"Well, you're welcome to check out any of mine whenever you want to."

She smiled. "Thanks. I just might take you up on that."

"Great."

"Well, I'll let you get back to reading your magazines, and I guess I will see you around sometime."

I quickly took out my cell phone. "Can I get your number? I could call you and maybe we could get together and hang out sometime—that is, unless you have other things going on in your life."

"I'd like that," she responded, taking out her cell phone, too. "You can just call my number so that yours will already be on my phone."

"Okay. I'm ready."

Her voice was almost melodic as she said each number slowly enough for me to have punched each one multiple times. "6-6-2-5-5-5-6-6-1-1."

I didn't think anything of the number until I called it back to her for confirmation. "Did you say 6-6-1-1?"

"Yeah."

The thought hit me so quickly that it almost knocked me off of my feet. "Who is your grandmother?"

"Anne Tibbs."

"Miss Anne?"

"Yeah."

I smiled, every tooth in my mouth pushing through.

"Nancy, do you have plans for dinner tonight?"

"Not really. I just need to check on my grandmother."

"You do that. And when you're free, give me a call. I'd love to take you out to dinner. Give you a proper welcome back to Daily, you know."

"I'd like that," she responded. "I'd definitely like that."

As I watched her walk away, I smiled and thought back to my exchange with Miss Anne. The numbers suddenly felt like the most valuable things in my possession.

I didn't know what would ultimately become of Nancy and me, but I did know one thing: whatever was going on across town at Tonya's wedding held little to no interest for me.

A Theory on Toilet Paper

Back during a period shortly after I had come to define dating as "the act of spending money in order to find out how little you have in common with someone," I had been given a bit of advice by my uncle, a street soothsayer named Mudbone, advice that, as was typical of the old man, had little to do with anything seemingly relevant, but always managed to find an eerie way of manifesting itself into situations that I would sometimes find myself.

That Uncle Mudbone opted to share with me his insights into toilet paper one day did not completely take me by surprise.

"Aaron, what kind of tissue do you use?" he had asked.

"What do you mean?"

"When you wipe your ass. What kind of tissue do you use?"

"Why do you ask?"

"I've been taking a poll."

I forced myself to keep from lifting my eyebrow in wonder. Instead I asked, "What have you found out so far?"

Mudbone smiled, revealing his large teeth, too white and straight to be his own. He loved it when I indulged him.

"For folks with low to no income, they use the single ply. It's the most affordable, but it ultimately provides the least protection. It's the closest thing to wiping your ass barehanded. Now, just because people don't have a lot of money don't mean they should have to wipe their asses barehanded."

I nodded, which incidentally encouraged him further.

"One wrong angle of the hand, and presto! You get what I call 'hammer hand.'"

"What's hammer hand?"

"It's where the edge of your hand along here," he responded, rubbing downward from his fifth finger, "gets soiled, despite your best efforts."

He looked up, noticing that I was still staring at the side of his hand, so he continued. "Then there's double-ply. But you have to be careful there. Some double-ply is just that weak ass single-ply clinging to another piece of single-ply."

"But isn't that what double-ply means?"

"Technically, which brings me to the quilted style, which is actually rather soft to the ass. It holds together really well, unlike that fuzzy ply that Cottonelle likes to sell. You can wipe with that stuff and get lint in your ass. Know what I'm saying?"

I nodded again, not because I agreed, but because I was actually becoming more impressed with his level of analysis, even in his somewhat inebriated state.

"You know," he continued, "I once had a conversation with a certified millionaire and he gave me a roll of the paper he uses. Oh my goodness! That stuff feels like you're wiping your ass with cashmere! I believe there were vitamins and minerals in there."

"So rich people have the best toilet paper?"

"Well, let me put it to you this way: if I was rich, I'd probably be wiping my ass right now instead of talking to you."

I had no idea that such a conversation would ever be relevant to my life, much less find its way into one of my dating scenarios, but, consistent with life's unpredictability, it did.

Her name was Jolie Soleil. Pretty Sun. No shit. While her mother was English, her father was from Senegal, and in an act odd by even Senegalese standards, he had given her both a first and last name, making Jolie the only one in her family with a different surname. But to her father's credit, he blessed her with a uniqueness that not many other women in Brooklyn had at that time. I dug her name, and with the lovely hue of her golden skin and curly brown hair, she was definitely the embodiment of such a name.

We met on a flight back from Atlanta to New York. I had just finished taking fall break at my sister's house in Marietta and was headed back to my grad school classes at Pace University to finish up the semester. Normally I would have slept on the plane because of a fear of turbulence I had acquired a while back. On this particular flight, however, I had trouble going to sleep, so I pulled a book from my computer bag.

Leaning down to grab the book, I noticed her, and my stomach turned into one big bubble gut. From that point forward I battled back and forth between whether or not I should try to strike up a conversation. I loathed the idea of being the creepy guy hounding her throughout the duration of the flight. Instead, I left her alone to enjoy the magazine she was reading. With the plane beginning to descend, I quickly reached for a napkin I had tucked away in the magazine pocket in front of me. With a kind of gross ferocity reserved primarily for scribblers of last minute poetry at open mics, I opened up the cloudy recesses of my brain and started jotting down what could best be called clichéd, desperate poetry, the kind of poetry a man claws for while trying to compose something for a woman he intends to give it to as soon as the pen is lifted from the paper. By the time the plane touched down and we were allowed to unfasten our seat belts, I had finished something that I hoped she would at least read, signing the napkin with both my name and phone number. If she called, she called; if she didn't, well, that was life. As she stood to retrieve her carryon bag, I gently placed the poem into her hand. She looked at me surprised I was giving her something. She smiled, folding the note in half and placing it in the purse that hung across her shoulder. In theory that should have been the last time that I saw her, but because the universe bends toward absurdity, two days later I was the recipient of a fortuitous call from a woman whose name I couldn't even pronounce at first.

After a week of late night phone conversations, I had primed the situation so that she would have trouble turning down an invitation to go out with me and spend a little time together. When she agreed, I considered the different places I could take her that would not break my student financial situation. After all, I had adopted a mantra about dating that was less than flattering. During that window of my life, I was opting for taking my female company to places that didn't require a lot of money to have a good time. The women who had the misfortune of going out with me during that period could put the blame on a woman named Yvette Whittington. That woman ran up a $159.96 bill at a restaurant she selected for me to take her to, and all of that was before the tip. After she waited for me to pay the bill, half of the food on her plate still staring us smack in our faces, she fell asleep on the drive home and told me a week later she was dating a guy who worked on Wall Street. So Jolie, who was a different personality altogether, would not see that side of things. We would have a nice, fun, inexpensive outing and when and if things picked up, we'd get to those joints much farther along.

On the day of our "date" I had a brief moment where Uncle Mudbone's theory of toilet paper filled my mind. With only a few squares left on the roll, I found myself doing a penguin waddle, pants cuffing my ankles like shackles, to the stash beneath the sink. This was how I dealt with calming my nerves, a practice some of my more graphic friends referred to as taking a nervous shit. Seeing the double-size roll of translucent single-ply made me realize something: I had a single-ply attitude about life. I was the kind of guy who sought out generic items to purchase everywhere I went for everything that I bought, although I could have easily afforded to go with brands of better quality. I shuddered at what Uncle Mudbone would think of my toilet paper choice.

Jolie and I met on Montague Street in Brooklyn Heights, just outside the train station. My plan was to take her to Haagen-Dazs (a splurge, I know) and get two cups of rich ice cream or sherbet and head down to the promenade where we would then sit on a bench and look at the Statue of Liberty and the skyline of the financial district across the East River, all while we got to know each other. My plan worked well, and with our appetites satiated, it was only a matter of how well our conversation went before we decided where to go next. It turned out that the next place was her apartment just off of St. Mark's Place in the East Village.

By the time we reached the steps of her brownstone, I knew something was wrong. At first I thought it was just the bubbleguts that accompanied any potential sexual encounter with someone new, but the more my stomach rumbled, I realized that I had miscalculated the entire evening. My stomach had begun to remind me that I was not as tolerant of lactose as I had let on earlier.

So there I was in Jolie's dimly-lit studio, the sounds of Sade pushing out from the speakers and this gorgeous woman sliding out of her shoes and snuggling against the pillows on her full-sized bed, the only real furniture in the small but well laid-out room.

"Aaron, you can have a seat," she said, her voice soft and as melodious as Adu's sweet alto pouring through the speakers.

I took a seat on the bed, laying my head back against the wall, my legs draped over the edge.

Placing her feet on my lap, she said, "You okay? You look a little tense."

"No, I'm good," I said, smiling, but my stomach was starting to make thick, churning sounds. "Guess I'm a little hungry though," I said, explaining away the gas that was building in my gut.

"You wanna send out for something?"

"I'm okay," I said. "You know, you are a very beautiful woman," I offered, hoping to change topics.

She smiled, blushing. "Thank you."

We were silent for a moment, smiling at each other.

"A penny for your thoughts?" I offered.

"I'm just thinking that I've never done anything like this before."

"Like what?"

"This. You know. Meeting a guy on an airplane and calling him after he hands me a poem. And here you are, sitting in my apartment now. It's all kind of funny."

"Yeah," I responded, shifting myself so that I didn't get completely choked out by a ball of gas building deep within the walls of my intestines. "I can't say I've ever done anything like this before either."

Jolie nodded her head, at first in agreement, then with the beat of the song. "I love Sade."

"So do I. Did you know Sade's actually a band?"

"Really?"

"Yeah, they took their name after the lead singer's name."

"Cool," she said, lifting her feet from my lap and standing up. She closed her eyes and began to sway her body with the music, and as the shadows danced over her body, I realized that she was a woman who was well aware of herself and her sensuality. More than anything I wanted to reach out and take her hand, pulling her close to me—but my stomach made it difficult to stand. My body wanted to fold up inside of the cramp that was forming.

"Dance with me," she said, extending her delicate fingertips toward me.

When I touched her hand and rose from my seated position, fear ripped through my mind quickly as I feared I would pass gas. I clinched up extra tight, biting my lip.

"Let me use the bathroom right quick. I wanna make sure I wash my hands, since we've been on the trains and stuff."

Jolie nodded her head. "Sure. The bathroom is right over there," she said, pointing to a door that I might have easily mistaken for a closet.

Now, exercising any reasonable degree of common sense, I would have never used the bathroom as a first-time visitor in a date's apartment, but I knew I would not last in my present state. The woman on the other side of the bathroom door was getting in the mood to be romantic, and all I could think about was getting out anything that was clogging up my ability to think straight. My mind flashed to Ben Stiller's mishap in *Along Came Polly*. I silently prayed that the same thing would not happen to me, and I did all of this praying while I unbuckled my pants and slid them down around my ankles. I glanced at the toilet paper roll just to make sure that she wasn't like me and prone to leaving a nearly empty roll hanging there to tease company. Reaching over blindly, I turned on the sink to what would have been full blast, had the water pressure been stronger. And then came the hard part: trying to ease out a little gas at a time so as to not make too much noise and alert her to my modus operandi. Her studio apartment was far too small to get away with much. Once I cracked the first one, my stomach got the notion that it was alright to right itself, and everything came out of me in a violent explosion, which would have been frightening had it not caused so much relief. I reached out my right hand and splashed it wildly beneath the water in the sink. It was important that she heard my hands under the water more than anything else, I figured. *Curse you, Ben Stiller!*

I could hear Sade through the door and only imagine Jolie moving her body to the syncopated rhythms of the music. The worst had passed, I figured, so I reached for the toilet paper. As my fingers tugged at the thick, soft squares, I thought about my own weak-ass toilet paper. This was the good stuff, the stuff that Uncle Mudbone had gone on about, and using it felt like I was pampering myself. When I finished and flushed, I stared at the toilet paper. Jolie used this stuff every day, and she probably used much more of it than I would. She was in a different league, and I couldn't even say that it was one I aspired to. She was the kind of woman who used the cashmere-esque toilet paper; I was but a lowly single-ply guy. I knew it would never work.

Not that she needed my input on that part anyway.

In my fascination with her toilet paper, I had failed to do something as basic as spray a bit of deodorizer before opening the door. The lights came on, the music stopped, and I found myself on the other side of her door, walking with the gentle breeze of St. Mark's Place, away from what would have surely been an exciting evening.

Sitting in the shadows of the subway station waiting for my train, my stomach rumbled again. *The good stuff*, I thought. I knew one day I would have to set my miserly ways aside and graduate to it, but that was far too easy.

I was the kind of guy who preferred adventure, and fewer things were more adventurous than narrowly avoiding "hammer hand."

16 Bars

When I revealed to my freshman composition class that I used to rock the mic as an emcee, nearly all of them doubled over laughing and slapping their desks. One kid even went as far as to ask permission to go to the restroom so he didn't piss himself from hysteria. I knew that they might find the idea of Professor Dennis with a high-top skin-fade and a gold rope amusing, but the wind from their laughter actually cut me a little. I continued on with my discussion about whether certain rappers should be included in our current literary canon, but even when I finished class, I could hear the resounding echo of their laughter still ringing in my ears. I wanted more than anything to show them that I had never been and would never be some wack dude in a tweed coat and tighty whiteys, completely out of touch with hip-hop.

As I slid my laptop into my book bag, I saw Noble Williams lingering behind the group exiting the room. He eased up to the desk, monster headphones resting around his thick neck and a slim notebook in his hand—no textbook to be found, and said, "Professor Dennis, you for real about being an emcee?"

"Yes," I responded. "I used to battle back in the day in Memphis."

"Yo, that's what's up. You think you still nice with yours?"

"Mr. Williams," I said, addressing him in the manner in which I had become accustomed to addressing my students, "I can definitely hold my own."

Noble nodded his head. "Well, yo, I got this mixtape I'm tryna throw up on the Internet in a few months. You wanna spit sixteen on a track?"

"Are you serious?" I responded, still trying to process his question. I hadn't rapped in any serious way since college, although I sometimes freestyled for my five-year-old daughter on our weekend drives. But flowing about Dora the Explorer was not what Noble was asking me to do.

"I'm just sayin," Noble started. "I think it'd be a good look to have my prof on a track letting loose. If you really about yours, folks ain't gonna laugh at you. That's my word."

Maybe it was the thought of silencing my students once and for all or maybe it was the desire to be hunkered over a microphone in a studio reliving my dreams from when I was younger, but whatever it was, I told him I would do it.

It wasn't until I got home and told my wife about it that I realized I might've been in over my head.

The ensuing conversation with my wife was comical in its brevity.

"Baby, should I do it?"

"Sure."

My wife had never heard me rap and didn't even know that I used to harbor fantasies of rocking the mic back in the day, years before I majored in English at FAMU and went on to grad school.

"What if I suck?" I asked.

"Then you'll just suck, and we'll move on."

If it weren't for her staring directly at me, holding one of my hands in hers as she said these things, I might have thought she was being dismissive of the whole thing. Even my daughter, Lena, smiled and clapped her hands when I told her that her daddy was going to be on a rap song.

Now I was definitely locked in, but I hadn't done my thing in so long I wondered if I could even do it anymore. That night I downloaded some instrumental tracks from some of my favorite rappers of the last three years, and sat down with one of my tablets trying to get some inspiration. What could I talk about? I was a husband, a father, and a teacher. I didn't think any of that would be what Noble was looking for, although I knew a lot of rappers were married with children. Back when I was rapping, we either rapped about our DJs or ourselves, pretty much the usual bragging about our own hotness or what neighborhoods we represented.

I knew up front I couldn't do anything hard edged because that wasn't me, so I scanned through music by the PhD kids, rappers whose mothers had doctorates, to see what they were talking about. So there I was, earbuds in my ears playing Mos, Talib, Common, and Kanye nonstop for the next three hours. The more I listened, the more I realized that it was much easier for me to analyze their lyrics than it was for me to write my own.

Two days later when my composition class ended for the day, Noble came back to me, a broad grin on his usually solemn face.

"You good, prof?" he asked.

"Yeah. How is everything with you?"

"Just trying to get this track together. You free this weekend? My boys and I got the studio on lock for a few hours and we wanna get some tracks laid."

The immediacy of it all caught me off guard, and I felt like I had just awakened to find myself standing on the ledge of a building. "Yes, I think I can get away for a few hours," I said, trying to ignore the numbness swarming over my legs.

"A'ight. We doin' this track about hoodin' and nerdin'."

"Like Lupe's 'I'm Beaming?'" I said.

Noble nodded his head. "That's what's up, prof. You know what I'm talkin' about. So just come prepared to spit sixteen bars on that."

I nodded, as if I did sixteen bars every day of my life and it was no big thing. Noble took a sheet of paper out of his bag and scribbled an address and cell phone number on it. "Come through around five, and we'll try to get you done first."

"Cool," I said.

He dapped me and walked out of the classroom. I had to admire his focus. He didn't say much in class, but he kept an "A" average. In fact, his work was among the best in the class, so I figured if he brought that same focus to his music, then he would set a pretty high bar for the song.

As I walked out of the room, I realized that there was a strong probability that I would be the weakest emcee on the track, and I couldn't go out like that. My father used to tell me whenever I went out of town on trips back in high school, "Don't do anything to embarrass yourself, your family, or the Black race." So I understood very clearly that whatever I did, I would have to at least represent on a level as to not embarrass Noble, myself, my wife and daughter, or my father. Oh yeah, and the Black race.

The very first time I battled another emcee was when I was in the eighth grade. Back then it wasn't about talent shows as much as it was about battling on the playground during recess. We would huddle in a group that would gradually expand as other people figured out what was going on. There was normally a neutral, respected beatboxer kicking the beat for all of the emcees, and we would stand toe-to-toe working either from memory or going completely off the dome. Some days you'd win; some days you'd lose. At nights, you'd just go back to your notebook and write some more rhymes, memorize them, get out on the playground the next day, and battle your ass off.

I did this all the way through high school, and when I went to college, I found a few other emcees and we would cipher deep into the night. I even thought a record deal might come out of all of it, but it never turned out that way. Instead, I parlayed my love of poetry into a thesis on the Harlem Renaissance and then a dissertation on Langston Hughes.

Now here I was in my home office with a notepad stretched out in front of me nodding to a Kanye West instrumental, earbuds sealed tightly in my ears. I didn't even notice my little girl walk up beside me with a small gift-wrapped box in her hands. I yanked the buds out of my ears and said, "Thank you, sweetie." I looked back and saw my wife standing in the doorway smiling.

"Open it, Daddy," Lena said, unable conceal her own smile.

I undid the package as carefully as I could while my daughter and wife waited patiently. When I lifted the lid on the box and saw a book that read *Rhyming Dictionary* inside, I grabbed my daughter and hugged her tightly. "Thank you, sweetie," I said.

I stood and walked over to my wife and gave her the kind of kiss that I normally reserved for her when we were in our bedroom.

"Ooooooh," Lena said. "Mommy and Daddy sittin' in a tree K-I-S-S-I-N-G!"

We turned to face our daughter and smiled sheepishly. Lena covered her mouth, giggling, but I could tell that she was happy to see her parents being romantic.

When they left me alone in the room with my new reference tool, I felt much better about the coming weekend. I had never used a rhyming dictionary, but the fact that my family had my back was far more important than any two words I could have strung together in verse.

On Saturday morning I hopped in the shower freestyling about anything I could think of, most of it just flat-out ridiculous. I even rhymed about the Axe shower gel I was using. Anything I could rhyme, I rhymed. By the time I finished breakfast with my family, I started getting ideas about what it was like growing up on the streets of Memphis and pushing myself to go to college at FAMU on scholarship just to get away from home. I grabbed my notepad and started jotting down ideas. Some of it was good, and some of it was definitely headed for the cutting room floor.

Throughout the day I tweaked my lyrics over and over until I thought I had something flexible enough for whatever beat Noble was going to throw at me. I quickly realized that my delivery style was a mixture of animation and seriousness, and I worried I would just sound like an old dude trying too hard. So I took my smartphone and started recording myself saying the words, trying different inflections and intonations. Every time I played back my sixteen bars, I flinched. I wasn't cut out for this. They would surely laugh at me and probably take me off the track altogether.

It seemed as if the more I practiced my rap, the worse I sounded, until finally I just took the sheet of paper and crumbled it up and threw it in the trash. Rather than waste any more time on this nonsense, I was going to go and see what was on cable. No sooner than I popped the leg rest on the recliner did my wife walk into the room.

"What are you doing?" she asked.

"I'm done. I can't do this anymore. I'm just not cut out for this. I'm not trying to play myself with these kids."

I could see the space between her eyebrows furrow, and I knew immediately that she didn't agree with my assessment. "But you've been working so hard."

"Baby, I'm thirty-eight. I have no business trying to bust a rhyme. I don't even sound right rapping. I sound like an Oreo," I said.

"A what?"

"An Oreo: black on the outside and white on the inside."

She shook her head. "No you don't. You sound like an intelligent, strong Black man," she said.

I smiled. "I know what you're doing. You're trying to do that Regina King/Cuba Gooding, Jr. thing on me from *Jerry Maguire*."

She chuckled softly before responding, "I love you, so I'm going to tell you the truth. If you were some wack brother, I wouldn't be with you."

I shrugged, picking the remote control back up off of the end table. "I could do a lot less damage just staying here today."

She walked over and stood between me and the television. "What made you say yes to this kid in the first place?"

I sighed. "I just wanted to show everyone that I still had it."

"And you don't want to do that any more?" she asked.

"No," I said, putting the remote control down.

"I don't blame you."

"So then we agree?" I said.

My wife shook her head. "No, actually we don't. The difference between you and me is that you think you should do this for other people, and I think you should do it for yourself."

I couldn't find the words to respond to her comment. Instead I sat there replaying her words in my mind. That's when Lena walked into the room singing Willow Smith's song "Whip My Hair."

My wife looked at me and then at our daughter. I turned off the television and looked down at my watch.

It was three o'clock. Clearly I had to get myself ready for my appointment at five.

In the drive over to the studio, I steadied my breath and cleared my head. My lyrics were in the garbage can back at home. I would be freestyling my sixteen bars today, and while I had no idea of how I wanted to start or end, whether I wanted to use metaphors or personification or any word play with homophones, I knew I was going to say whatever was on my heart. I remembered what it was like to stand in the battle huddles in junior high, what it felt like to be sitting in the dorm kicking sixteen bars around the cipher circle at two in the morning, what it felt like to hear a J. Dilla track for the first time, and what it felt like to hear The Legendary Roots Crew rock a crowd in a small Philly club.

When I walked through the door of the studio, Noble dapped me and introduced me around.

"You ready?" he asked.

"About as ready as I'll ever be," I responded.

He showed me to the recording booth, and I put on the headphones that were wrapped around the microphone stand.

"We'll play the track a few times for you, and you can see how your lyrics fit with the beat before we record."

"Okay," I said, as the engineer turned on the music in my headphones. I could feel the beat moving in my chest, the bassline expanding in my head. I couldn't place the track, but I could tell the sample was from Earth, Wind & Fire. I closed my eyes and cleared my head. After a minute, I said, "I'm ready."

Noble said, "Word? You write your stuff down?"

"No, I'm going off the dome."

"That's what's up," he said, nodding his head.

We did a mic check to make sure the levels were right and that my voice was picking up properly, and then Noble left for the engineering booth.

Alone in the recording booth for the first time, the beat still moving through my head, I smiled. I was actually here—after all of this time. This was what I had always wanted. This was my chance to put a creative piece of myself into existence.

I could hear Noble in my headset. "We're about to drop the beat. Just come in when you're ready."

My mind was as clear as the waters of the Caribbean. I inhaled, the beat enveloping me like the embrace of a long-lost lover. The bassline moved like a jump rope being swung widely in an arc, inviting me.

I leaned forward, opened my mouth, and jumped in.

Dogs and Bullets

Twenty years ago, while drunk off their asses at the county bar association Christmas party, the then twenty-three lawyers in attendance took a straw poll to see which of them was the most likely to get shot by a disgruntled client. The group unanimously selected Grey Alexander, mainly because he was a criminal lawyer notorious for blowing off clients who had trouble paying their legal fees on time—and Grey *did* get shot in the leg three years later by a recently released client who hadn't found it funny when Grey handed him a bar of soap that read DO NOT DROP, just moments after the verdict was announced—but so did two other lawyers, one who didn't survive and one who did. The one who didn't survive, Larson Evers, fired the .44 Magnum himself, and the one who *did* survive, Grady Sails, would one day become my boss.

Grady had been practicing law since way back before I was born, and he had been the attorney for my family up until my father and mother decided to retire to the south of Florida. I grew up around Grady, but if you had asked me what I wanted to be when I grew up, it definitely wouldn't have been a lawyer. Grady was the only one that I knew, and while I thought he was a good enough person (from what I could gather as a kid), I didn't much like the idea of sitting around an office all day wearing a suit and tie and signing papers.

In fact, if I were to be absolutely honest, I would have to say that the only thing that really impressed me about Grady *was* the fact that he had been shot. Back then, not many people in Mississippi were getting shot, so knowing someone who had gotten shot at all was a big thing, but knowing someone who had *survived* being shot meant that you had a story that all of the other kids on the block would envy. Grady was that for me—an anecdote—and as I got older, in my mind he became a kind of hero. After all, he had stared death in the face and laughed. Or so I thought.

I wouldn't find out what really happened until I started working for Grady. He referred to it as the Mourning case. The case involved a guy named Dennis Mourning who was in a car accident (not his fault, according the accident report) and his pick-up truck was crushed like an accordion, breaking his leg clean in two. Three days later, after treating with a local doctor, Mourning was in his den watching television when he found that he couldn't breathe. He died before he made it to the hospital.

The autopsy concluded that it was a pulmonary embolism resulting from deep vein thrombosis, so

Grady did what any decent lawyer would do: he filed
the lawsuit in the predominately black county in which
the accident took place and proceeded to sue everyone
from the driver to the automobile manufacturer to the
doctor. This was in the heyday of mass tort litigation,
and Grady was able to successfully settle all of the cases,
combined, for just north of three and a half million
dollars a few days before the trial was to start.
Mourning's oldest son, after doing the math and seeing
just how much the contingency fee would be on a
settlement of that size, simply decided that Grady was
being paid too much. It didn't matter that Grady had
opted to cut his fee down to 33% (a fee he typically
reserved for only non-litigated cases—which this one
had not been); all that seemed to matter was that the
Mourning family wanted as much money as they could
get their hands on. When Grady declined to cut his fee
any further, the oldest Mourning boy (who was roughly
sixteen) walked into the law office with a .22 caliber
pistol, pointing it at him. Grady laughed, grabbed the
pistol from the nervous boy's hand and tossed it on his
desk. The gun discharged when it hit the desk, and
Grady looked down and realized that his arm was
bleeding. Rather than be embarrassed by the mishap, he
actually started rolling up his sleeves on every occasion
so the scar on his left forearm could be prominently
displayed.

That was Grady for you.

"Paul, what was the lesson to that story?" Grady
asked me during one of our weekly one-on-ones.

"Don't grab a gun out the hands of another person?"

"No, son," he responded. "Don't throw a loaded gun on a desk."

I could only nod. I don't know if I was cut from a different cloth, but if someone entered my office with a gun, the last thing I would be thinking about is grabbing *or* throwing the damn thing. But knowing Grady like I do, the gun was probably a metaphor, and whatever lesson he was trying to teach me would have to sink in much later.

My office faces due west, so from my window I can see the still active railroad tracks that cut right down through the small town of Daily, Mississippi. Roughly once a week I hear the short and long blasts of a train. While something like that might serve as a distraction to Northern lawyers, like my classmates from the National Law Center in DC, I find it refreshing to see the train cars pushing along slowly, the wheels squealing, yearning to move faster than the town will allow. A national magazine once called Daily one of the most beautiful small towns in America and even went so far as to say Daily was a living, breathing Norman Rockwell painting. But Daily is far from a Norman Rockwell painting, once you get past the repainted buildings downtown and the lush antebellum style houses lining Main Street. It is a beautiful, but dark place, more like Grace Metalious's Peyton Place than Andy Griffith's

Mayberry. The great, late poet Aleda Shirley once said it best: "I have a love/hate relationship with Mississippi." Those are my sentiments exactly. While there are things that I hate about my town and my state, I would not want to trade these Southern nuances for the hustle and bustle of a big city up North. I guess at heart I'm just a Southern boy.

I return my eyes to the four-inch case binder on my desk. This litigation notebook has been the bane of my existence since I inherited it from another lawyer who left the firm, moved to the next county over, and started a competing personal injury practice. It screams volumes that she didn't take this case with her.

After pouring over a deposition taken nearly two years ago, I immediately recognize this case for what it is: a dog—which is contrary to what Grady wants me to believe it is. I am the youngest and newest of the four lawyers at this firm, and common sense would dictate that if there was any real money in this thing, it would not have been handed down to me like a skunk soaked in chitterling juice. I glance out the window again, secretly hoping to hear the blasts of a train or see something that would help unclog my constipated mind. This client, whom I have never met, will be in this afternoon for an update, and I have contemplated returning the file so the person can take it to another lawyer, one who might not mind taking on a dog of a case.

Grady drops by my office just before lunch.

"I see that Miss Griggs is coming in this afternoon," he says.

"Yes. I was just going over her file."

"To tell the truth, we should've already gone to trial on this a long time ago. I didn't know how much foot dragging Amina had done on this file before she left. Let's see if we can get something moving on this soon."

"Can I speak to you off the record for a moment?" I ask.

"Sure, Paul," he says, stepping all the way into my office and closing the door behind himself.

"I've been over this file a hundred times, and I'm convinced that we need to just give this file back to her. This thing is a mess. Look at the facts. She stumbles in the parking lot of Rotor Sam's in a spot that can't be any more open and obvious than if you shined a spotlight on it. On top of that, she tells the first witness—the one we deposed years ago— that she tripped over her own feet. It took six months for her to even tell anyone that she believed the sun reflecting off of the concrete kept her from seeing the hole. Add on to that the fact that the main part of her medical bills is the ambulance ride to the hospital—oh yeah, and the x-ray that came up clean. The rest of these bills are chiropractic appointments that could have been for anything under the sun. Be honest, this case is a dog, isn't it?"

Grady smiles. I expect him to nod or shake his head, but he does neither.

"If it was a dog, do you think it would have stayed in the office this long?"

"Truthfully? Yes."

Again he smiles.

"I tell you what. Meet with Miss Griggs first, and we can pick back up on this conversation later."

I sigh. "I don't think that will change anything."

"Maybe. Maybe not. But don't you feel you at least owe it to your client to talk to her directly about her case?"

I feel like he is guilting me at this point. Of course I'm going to meet with her, but as a professional, I have to already know what my primary options are. Isn't that what thinking like a lawyer really means? Removing emotion and making a focused and intelligent legal decision?

"I'll meet with her, and we can see what happens," I say, more for his benefit than my own.

"Sounds good to me," he says, opening my door, nodding to me, and walking away.

I stare at the case binder again, all four inches of paperwork: discovery responses and documents, depositions, photographs, medical records and bills, and statements of admission. I feel as though I know this woman's life story from having reviewed all of this stuff numerous times and that meeting with her is just a formality.

Grady doesn't need to call it a dog. If it barks and wags its tail like one, that's all I need to know.

Miss Griggs arrives ten minutes before her appointment, so I have Vanessa, our receptionist, go ahead and escort her to the larger of our three conference rooms. I am just finishing up a conversation with an insurance adjuster on a case that actually *does* have some value, but I walk over to the conference room as soon as I finish. It's not so much that I don't want her to wait as it is my wanting to get this over with as quickly as possible.

The first thing I notice about Miss Griggs as I walk through the door is that she is small and round, like a ball with arms and legs. She is not even five feet, and the roundness of her body is surprisingly symmetrical, her breasts and stomach all smoothly blended into one impressive sphere. The frames of her glasses are round, complementing her salt and pepper Afro. She is clearly a study in circles.

From her file I know she is fifty-seven. I even know her weight, as well as most of the major health issues she has had in the last ten years, none of which appear to have been aggravated by her fall, unless you read a few years of chiropractic adjustments into the equation and ignore the fact that she has degenerative disc disease.

"Hi, Attorney Thomas," she says, rising from her seat and extending a plump hand. Her smile is infectious, and I smile in return.

"How are you doing this afternoon, Miss Griggs?"

She takes her seat carefully, trying to avoid grimacing, but in that single moment, I can see that this woman is in pain and that she apparently has been wrestling with it for a while.

"I'm blessed," she says. Relief spreads over her face as she takes a seat.

"I've been studying your file for the past few weeks, and it's good to finally meet you in person."

"Yes, sir."

It feels funny, this older woman calling me "sir" when she is nearly thirty years my senior, and I start to tell her so, but I decide not to bother.

"So how is my case going?" she asks. Her face is hopeful, and I feel guilty telling her that her file doesn't look worthwhile at this point.

"Well," I start, "things have been moving pretty slowly, and we are still working to get the pre-trial conference set."

"What does that mean?"

"It means that I will meet with the other lawyer and the judge, and we'll set some deadlines for wrapping up the discovery and trying the case. Once we're on the calendar, the next stop will be the trial."

"Do you think my case will settle?"

I look into her eyes, and I can see that she desperately wants me to tell her that it will, but my tongue is stingy with the words.

"I don't see anything in the file that shows that we are in position to settle this. I'll keep trying though."

"Will you, please?" she asks. "I don't wanna go to court."

"I'll see what I can do." I don't mention that I don't want to go to court on these facts either.

I try explaining to her some of the weaknesses of her case and what the discussions with the defense attorney have been like so far. It's not looking like this case will be easy to settle, I tell her. We have an uphill battle that might be insurmountable should we make it to a jury, I say.

"But there's still a chance, right?" she asks.

Her eyes are round behind her glasses, and for a moment, she looks like one large smile.

"There's always a chance," I offer.

She nods enthusiastically.

"Okay," I say. "You know, I have gone through all of the depositions and everything, but I just want to hear, in your words, what happened on the day that you fell."

Miss Griggs leans forward, interlocking her fingers, and begins to describe the day of the fall: the time, location, weather conditions, and what happened afterwards.

"You told the first witness, Janice Carver, that the sun had gotten in your eyes and that you had tripped over your own feet," I tell her.

"Yeah."

"Was there any particular reason you told her that, if you felt that it was the hole in the concrete that tripped you?"

She shakes her head slowly and says, "I was embarrassed."

"Embarrassed?" I repeat.

"Attorney Thomas, my whole life I've been big-boned—and I ain't that tall, as you can probably see. People been picking on me most of my life. Anytime something happens to me, people laugh at me. It makes me not want to do anything that'll make people stare. When I saw that woman after I busted my ass on that concrete, I felt so shame-faced. The only thing going through my head was that this woman was gon' laugh at me. I just wanted her to get out of my face, so I said the first thing that came to my mind. But for real, I felt my foot catch on something, and I swear I didn't see it. And I usually notice stuff on the ground, because I walk with my head down a lot. One second I was walking, and the next second I was on the ground."

"Why isn't this information in your deposition?" I ask.

"I don't remember what I said at the deposition. That was a long time ago."

I take out a copy of her deposition and thumb through the 88 pages to a page where I remember having seen her comment. I read her response. "You say here, 'I didn't realize why I fell until I went back to Rotor Sam's later and saw there was a hole in the concrete near where I fell.'"

"I said that?"

"Yes, you did. Under oath, too."

"So what does that mean?"

"The defense attorney will probably try to make you look like a liar to the jury for not saying what really happened when he took your deposition."

She lowers her head, considering this. The look of sadness on her face is very awkward and inconsistent with her appearance. I want to say something to her to raise her spirits, but I don't want to raise her expectations in the process.

"Well, have they offered any money at all since the last time?"

"No. They've only offered $800, and that was back before the case went into litigation. That doesn't even touch your medical bills or the amount of work we've put into discovery on this case. That amount they offered may as well be zero—or a negative, when you think about our office expenses."

It's my guess that if the previous attorney on this case would have known what the deposition would reveal, she might have considered whether it was even worthwhile to file suit in the first place.

Miss Griggs purses her lips tightly, moving them from side to side as she ponders this. "So we not going to be able to settle, and we ain't gonna win at trial either?"

"I didn't say either of those things. I'm just trying to get you to see the full picture, so you'll understand what we're up against."

"Well, Attorney Thomas, I don't know nothing about this law stuff, so I'm gonna ask you. What should I do?"

The answer to her question is already resting on my tongue, but I freeze up when I see her grimace and adjust herself in the chair.

"Do you need to stand up and stretch your back?" I ask.

"Yes, sir," she says, steadying herself and pushing upward. With her hands on her hips, she walks around the seat slowly.

Seeing her move, I ask, "Are you on disability?"

"I applied, but they rejected me, so I just sent in my application again."

I nod. "They'll probably reject you again because of how the system is set up, but if you want, I can help you to appeal your case."

"So do I have to sign anything with you?"

"Not now. Let's wait and see if they approve you on the second application. If they do, then you won't need me. If they don't grant your disability, I'd be happy to talk with you about your case and sign you up, if you need a representative."

"Thank you," she says, slowly easing herself back into her chair. "So what should I do about this case that you're working on now?"

I inhale deeply, considering my thoughts. "I'll call the other attorney this afternoon and see if anything has changed on our settlement possibilities. We can just start there, and then we'll know what your options are at that point. Let's just wait and see what happens."

"Okay," she responds. I know this is not what she wants to hear, but her face holds tight to the optimism that seems so fleeting in this room.

As I walk her to the front door to meet her ride home, I promise to call her again with any updates before the week is out. She thanks me, and I return to my office in the back of the building, sitting down behind the case folder on my desk.

I hear Grady down the hall talking to one of the other lawyers in the firm, and I think back to when I was a child who looked up to him. Back then the practice of law was something magical and pure. It was something where black and white were clearly defined and the truth was always somewhere out there waiting to be discovered. Now things are as gray as Grady's hair, and I don't know how to feel about anything at any given moment. I am a lawyer, not the ultimate judge of people, and while I know what position I am supposed to be playing, sometimes I don't know exactly where on the field I should stand.

I lift the receiver from my phone and cradle it against my ear and shoulder. As I stare at the edge of my desk, I imagine Grady and the Mourning boy from all of those years back, the two of them fighting with a gun, both of them probably more afraid than they would have ever admitted to the other. I wonder what the Mourning boy did when he saw all of that blood. The story never really went that far. It was an anecdote, after all, and in an anecdote, we don't follow the antagonist home to watch him wrestle with his emotions over seeing a man get shot. Instead, he becomes "that client who did that thing that time."

As I look at Miss Grigg's file, I think about her low self-esteem and begin to feel sorry for her and what she has had to endure throughout her life. I understand why she dreads going to trial, but I also want her to see that she doesn't need to cower in the shadows of justice when she's the one who's been wronged. Then I realize that it's my job to stand up for her, not watch as she gets kicked around. It's an epiphany of the obvious, but I welcome it.

I open the file to the tabbed correspondence section and find the phone number of the defense attorney. I have no idea if this case will settle or if I will even be able to get Miss Griggs disability at the end of the day, but I know that it's my responsibility to give it my best shot.

I punch in the number and wait for the phone to ring. I take a long deep breath, clearing my head and focusing on the case. I'm going to get my client something for her troubles, I tell myself.

When the receptionist answers and switches me to the attorney's direct line, I cuff my sleeves to the elbows. I may not have a bullet scar on my forearm, but I am definitely prepared for battle.

Discovering Charles Buckner

I've heard it referred to as the "quicksand effect." That's when you find yourself so mired down in something that you can't do anything but watch everything go to shit in what seems like slow motion, just like watching a car wreck using the freeze-frame option on a DVD remote control. That's been my life since as far back as I can remember. I wish there was some exact point in my life that I could point to and say, "That's it! That's where it all started going downhill," but in all honesty, I've probably been on this very path since birth. I mean, how else can you explain a thirty-year-old grown-ass man living in the basement of his grandma's house. I have been an office temp for so long that I can scarcely remember what it was that I spent six years of college trying to achieve in the first place. Even more, and this is the really tragic part, I have not been out on a date since my high school senior prom, an event I would have attended stag had not my aunt gotten one of her friend's daughters to agree to go with me. The prom picture hanging in a frame on the wall of my room says it all: two heavyset brown-skinned kids looking more like brother and sister than lovers, both with expressions on their faces to suggest that they had just had a fight over that last Twinkie, and the prize had been smushed in the process.

While I don't really go out much, I have managed to create a minor presence on a few social websites like www.blackfolkhookup.com, where my handle is Black-Pantha, a reference to my favorite comic book hero. It took a little creative camera positioning, lighting, and Photoshop enhancement to get a picture that I felt would work, but I've managed to make a few friends whom I chat with on occasion. I haven't met any of them in person though. I just don't know what I would say if I were to meet any of these women. I've gotten used to being socially awkward at home with the few people I know, but I don't think I could stand the idea of letting someone I just physically met get her hopes dashed so quickly.

I've always expected that someone would take pity on me and maybe sit down and bless me with some knowledge on how to deal with women. It hasn't happened in thirty years, and I have all but lost hope that it will happen now.

As I sit looking at the calendar on my desktop computer, knowing that my thirty-first birthday is coming up in another week, I want to do something, *anything*, to reverse this painful downward spiral. If I had the money to move, I would have been out of my grandma's house a long time ago, and if I were in much better shape, I might have dated a little. My uncle Eldrick says that women are giving it away for free these days, but even if I believed him, I couldn't take letting a woman see me in the buff. I've looked at myself in the mirror, and I have so many grooves, stretches, and dents in my body that I couldn't possibly live down the kind of insult that I'm likely to get from a woman. Even more, I think I'd just crawl into a ball and die if she remarked that my tits were bigger than hers.

I look at the clock on my screen, and my stomach growls like a fourth grade trombone player. It's nearly ten in the morning, and since it's been pretty quiet for the past hour, I'm guessing that I'm the only one in the house right now. I figure since I don't have to do any temping today, I will pay a visit to Perry's Diner for the Tuesday lunch special. They have this incredible Salisbury steak! I feel my mouth watering just thinking about those savory sautéed mushrooms in that creamy gravy, cushioned with billowy mashed potatoes, salted just right, and a large glass of syrupy sweet iced tea.

I grab my coat and check myself in the mirror. I'm neat; my hair is brushed to hook up some waves, and my button-up is tucked into my khakis. I smile at the face looking back at me, and my stomach starts to tense up. Just the thought that Maya Smith could be working today makes me really nervous. She is the kind of fine that leaves my mouth dry, searching for even simple phrases. Just the thought of her makes me detour to the bathroom to see if I can alleviate some of that pressure off of my guts.

It's hard to eat when you're nervous.

Taking a seat at my favorite table in the diner, I don't even bother looking at the menu. In fact, shortly after I take my seat, I see Maya walking toward my table with a large glass of sweet tea in hand. She places it on the table in front of me, and I try to conceal my smile. For the past month, she has done this. In one respect, I am flattered by the fact that she can anticipate my order, but on the other hand, I am horrified that I have come across as so utterly predictable to such a beautiful woman.

She smiles and asks, "Charles, you want the special today, right?"

"Uhh. Yes. The Salisbury steak with mashed potatoes."

"Okay. It'll be up in a few."

"Thanks," I respond.

She walks away, and I observe the sweet, sway of her walk. Her waitress uniform comes right above the knee, and through her black stockings, I can see the nice fullness of her legs. She's what most guys would call "thick" because she has a little meat on her bones. She is so fine, with her peach-colored self! And she has one of the most beautiful faces I have ever seen. The only thing that keeps me going on days like this is to see that there's no ring on her left hand. Sometimes I imagine asking her out, but I doubt that I'll ever do that. Sometimes the fantasy is all you have, and it's better to keep that than to forfeit it for the truth.

I open the wrapped napkin holding my silverware and place each piece parallel to the other on the right side of the table. The emerald colored Formica tabletop has a tranquilizing effect as I stare at it. I drum my fingertips across the surface and find myself playing the haunting rhythm of Screamin' Jay Hawkin's "I Put a Spell On You." At that moment I imagine what it would be like to conjure such a spell over the likes of Maya Smith. The thought is so intoxicating that I barely notice her placing the Salisbury steak on the table in front of me. I muster a smile as she asks me if I need anything else. I want to say, "Your phone number," but that is far too corny to say, so I say nothing and shake my head.

The Salisbury steak is tender and juicy, separating easily as I push my fork through it. The thick gravy runs into my mashed potatoes, and I take a chunk of the meat and wipe it around deliciously in the potatoes before putting it into my mouth. For a moment I just hold the food on my tongue, savoring the seasonings. It's so good that I find myself nodding my head to this inaudible rhythm in my head, an action my cousin Charlene refers to as "the good food" dance. Within minutes, my plate is clean, and I am sipping large gulps of the iced tea, using that sweetness to balance the saltiness on my palate.

Sitting back, I look out over the restaurant. Only a handful of customers are scattered throughout the small diner, probably on their lunch breaks from the tax service directly across the street. I glance at my watch and see that it's a quarter to noon. I imagine more people will begin pouring in within the next twenty minutes, so I pick up my lunch ticket and head for the register.

As I reach in my pocket to pull out the money for my meal and tip, I see Maya gliding over to the register.

"How was your meal?" she asks. Her smile is so beautiful that it takes me a moment to collect myself and answer.

"Great! Absolutely delicious!" I respond a little too enthusiastically. "And you were a very good server." The last comment feels corny as it comes out of my mouth, but her smile holds firm.

I hand her the money, and she thanks me, telling me to come again. Just then I feel the sweet tea beginning to push on my bladder, so I open the door right next to the counter that leads to the men's and women's restrooms. I walk through the first door into a common area where the men's restroom door is on the left and the women's restroom door is on the right. The restroom is very clean for the restaurant to have been open since breakfast.

When I am finished, I wash my hands and pull down a few sheets of paper towel before opening the door. As I step into the common area, I hear the sound of yelling and screaming. I freeze in my tracks, straining to hear.

A man's voice is barking loudly and, with the exception of a handful of screams, the room is extremely silent. I look around me, and I realize that I am alone in here. Only a door separates me from whatever is going on out there, and I feel the overwhelming urge to sneak back into the restroom and climb upon one of the toilets to hide in one of the stalls. Instead, I lean forward placing my ear to the wall. The voice is directly on the other side of the wall, and it's only one voice. Someone is robbing the restaurant. If I just hold tight for a few minutes, everything will hopefully blow over, but then I remember Maya's smile. She was working the register just a few moments ago. She could still be there at gunpoint or something.

I ease around and place my hand against the door, which pushes outward. I part the door very slowly until I can catch a sliver of a view. It's almost like a bad joke: a clumsy looking man wearing a stocking over his face holding something out in front of him that I can't quite make out. I know it's a gun though. I strain a little bit more and see that there are people lying on the floor and the only other person standing is Maya, one of her hands raised out of fear as the other one grabs at cash in the register.

My heart is racing a hundred miles a minute, and when I notice the proximity of the guy's back to the door, I suddenly feel as if my legs will give out. I can feel my breaths coming short and quick, short and quick. I can no longer feel my hands resting against the door. And I don't know what happens in my head, but I suddenly throw all of my weight against the door, as if I'm trying to break it down. The door explodes open and slams directly into the back of the guy with the stocking over his face.

"Ugh," he grunts, as his hands fly up in pain and the gun falls from his hand and onto the floor.

I run over to him and throw my body over his in an effort to pin him down. Well, it's actually more like collapsing on him. Trying to catch my breath, I stretch my girth to smother the man with all of my being. While I am lying on the man's back as he struggles beneath me, one of the other customers retrieves the gun. I can hear Maya calling the police department right down the street, and I realize that it will all be over in minutes.

Still dazed from just giving my statement to the police, I barely hear Maya's voice.

"Charles?"

"Yes," I say, turning to face her.

"That was a very brave thing you just did."

I smile and lower my head, not wanting her to see my blushing.

"I hope you come back soon," she says.

"Yeah," I respond. "And I won't come back just for the Salisbury steak special!"

Just then I realize what I've just said. I brace myself.

"Good."

She leans over and kisses my cheek, and my stomach dances as if she just tickled my navel. Her words are soft. "I feel safer when you're around."

I have never heard those words before, but now I find myself wanting to expand to fit them. The funny thing is that I feel the process has already begun.

Black Hand Side

I had been dapping Kirby for four hours straight, and now all I wanted to do was just slap him in his bug-eyed face. My hand was tired and on the verge of cramping up like an arthritic crustacean claw.

"One more time, man," he said, massaging the palm of his dapping hand with his other hand.

I shook my own hand, flexing it and wriggling my fingers. "Okay, but just one more time. I don't think I have anything left."

"A'ight. Go all in this time."

"Kirb, I've been goin' all in the entire time. You just handle *your* business. You were a little sloppy on those last few moves."

Kirby grimaced. "Yeah, I know, man. My fingers are sticking a little on the end."

"Don't sweat it," I offered. "The competition is in two days. Just get a hand massage tomorrow morning and don't do anything until the competition. So no spanking the monkey or any of your other hobbies. This thing is no joke."

Kirby laughed, but he knew I was telling the truth. This dude really needed to learn to be a bit more ambidextrous in his extracurricular activities, because he was starting to look like that kid from M. Night Shyamalan's *Lady in the Water*, all diesel on one side and scrawny on the other.

I counted us off and we went into the handshake for the umpteenth time.

The judges would be evaluating us on originality, intricacy of movements, dexterity, enthusiasm, and smoothness. Each of the categories clearly had a subjective component to it, but a few minutes of watching past winners on YouTube gave us all an idea of what the standard was. In fact, if you still had plans to compete after seeing some of the dudes on those videos, then maybe you really were cut out for it. Most people just gave up and threw in the towel, Sonny Liston bailing out on the corner stool.

Kirby was slightly better the last time, but we still weren't on a Jedi-level with our moves yet. There were a few levels of stank we could still throw on our moves, but we could save those for the actual competition, I figured.

"This is gonna be our year," Kirby said. "People been blowing up my Vine account all week nut-cruising the sample I posted on Monday."

"I told you about posting our stuff on the Net. People'll jack your stuff if you put it out there."

"I only put like seven seconds for the loop."

I shook my head. "How much you wanna bet some wack team is gonna use that in their routine, though?"

"But we got two minutes of material. Seven seconds ain't gonna kill us."

"It better not," I said.

That was Kirby's problem: feeling the need to post everything online. He couldn't eat a spoonful of cornflakes without feeling the need to report it to his legion of followers. Still, I couldn't get too angry with him; after all it was his incessant posting that got us noticed and invited to the Dap Invitational in the first place. In fact, the buzz on social media was that we were among the favorites to take the Big Grip Award this year, the Dap Invitational's version of the Best Picture Oscar.

I told Kirby we'd connect the next afternoon and head on over to Memphis and check into our hotel. He nodded. I nodded.

It was a peace out without the dap. We had to save that for the competition.

That night I had a dream my hand was stuck in a silkworm web, and I kept trying to get it free, but the more I moved it, the more my fingers got tangled in it. Finally, I just started shaking my wrist trying to break free, but my hand was wrapped in white strands like the countrified version of a Michael Jackson glove.

I woke up in the middle of the night swatting my hand back and forth, still feeling the tickle of mummylike threads sweeping across my skin. It was official: my nerves were a mess.

The Dap Invitational was the major leagues, and for small town Mississippi boys like Kirby and me, this was what we needed to put ourselves on the map. If we won this thing, we could get in music videos and maybe a few commercials. Two years earlier a fast-food chain signed a contract with the winners—which is how most of us got exposed to the competitive level of dapping in the first place.

I remember the first time I saw competitive dapping. The first thing I thought was that I could do it blindfolded with a hand tied to an ankle behind my back. It was the most basic greeting used by black people the world over, so there was hardly anything special about it. The only people completely mystified by the art of dapping were white people who tended to vacillate between standard handshakes and enthusiastic high fives.

Of course my first assessment was a bit oversimplified. Sure, most black people coded daps into their greetings on the regular, but very few people took the time to choreograph intricate hand maneuvers that lasted for more than a few seconds. The average competitive dapper had routines around two minutes, which was actually a part of the guidelines issued by The Dap Invitational. After a little research I discovered that they had to implement the time limit five years ago after a team from Decatur, Georgia, cycled out a "looper" handshake for almost an hour. A looper was when a

handshake repeated over and over after a certain
number of movements. This was banned by The Dap
Invitational, alongside encrypted gang handshakes,
which were immediate grounds for disqualification.

Kirby had become my partner, mainly because he
was the smoothest dapper I knew in my immediate
circle. He could make some of the trickiest moves seem
like they were effortless. Kirby was to dapping as
Michael Jackson was to moonwalking. And he took it
seriously, too, which appealed to me, since I wanted to
team up with someone who had a hunger on par with
my own.

When we first started practicing, he would have his
hands moisturized to high heaven with some
dermatologist-recommended collagen-based cream that
made his hands sticky and clammy. I had to shut that
down immediately. For hands to move efficiently, there
needed to be some sense of friction present, and his
heavily hydrated hands, while full of dexterity, were
freakish in nature when you had to interact with them
for longer than two seconds. It felt like his hands had
been sweating. But he later took to covering his hands
in talcum powder before practice, his compromise with
me, since he had no plan to stop greasing himself up. I,
on the other hand, would hit my hands with a little
Purell ahead of time, so by the time I got to practice, my
skin had dried a little to give me a little ash, which was
always good for friction.

After a half hour, I lay back down and closed my tired eyes. *No silkworms*, I thought, moving my fingers rhythmically against the sheets. *No silkworms*. Please.

Memphis was not the Promised Land, but it was a step towards it.

I imagined Kirby and myself one day on the largest, grandest stage, elevated before the world, our brand of Negro Exoticism the flavor du jour, the toast of Parisians and Amsterdamians alike. We would be analogous to the South Korean b-boys who routinely whipped the world's collective ass in international break dance competitions.

As we drove up I-55 North listening to Big K.R.I.T. (our theme music for getting ourselves hype), I noticed Kirby in the passenger seat of my hatchback, his hands covered in gloves like Rogue from The X-Men. The way he held them to his chest was as if he were preparing for surgery. I could picture him saying, "We need 50 cc's of saline. She's crashing!"

"How are your hands feeling?" I asked.

"They feel real good, man. We're gonna kill it. Trust me."

"That's what I wanna hear."

I moved my fingers in rhythm across the steering wheel. My hands felt loose and easy. I had almost decided against getting my hands massaged earlier that morning, but it proved to be a good move after all. I figured I was as good to go as I would ever be. It was just too bad that we had to wait one more day to show our stuff.

"You know what's funny about The Dap Invitational?" Kirby asked.

"What?"

"It's, like, the last bastion of blackness left for us. Everything else has been taken over by other ethnic groups. When the Belgians won the Spades Open Tournament or when the Vietnamese took us to the bank in dominoes, or even the Chinese sealing the deal at the Cee-lo Tournament, black people have been losing out on stuff we used to dominate. It's like there's an Eminem or Yao Ming in every black game the world over."

"Well, the name Cee-lo actually comes from the Chinese."

"Man, how do you know all this miscellaneous stuff?" Kirby said, shaking his head. "You know what I mean, though. Hell, if there was a big dick contest, someone not black would take that, too."

I laughed. "You remember that video of the tribal dude wrapping his johnson around a pole and lifting boulders and stuff with it?"

"No way! I don't think I could handle that. There're just some things that shouldn't be attempted."

While we laughed, I could understand what Kirby was getting at. Still, it seemed inevitable that someone from a different ethnic group would eventually win even The Dap Invitational. It had yet to happen, but that only meant that the sport was primed for a "first."

"Well, if we're the best," I said, "then we shouldn't have anything to worry about, right?"

Kirby nodded.

We drove on to the hotel, each of us imagining ourselves standing on the first place platform waiving the giant $50,000 check before the news cameras.

It was our time—and we knew it.

We were perfect.

Every finger in sync.

Our arms were fluid extensions of hands that were married in movement like mating eagles falling from the heavens.

It was like we invented dapping, like we were the true originators of the art.

That's what made our loss so confounding.

To add salt to the wound, the Big Grip Award winners of The Dap Invitational were a group of countrified white boys from Kentucky. Those guys actually showed up with sleeveless white t-shirts featuring the Confederate flag, their pants sagging off their asses, revealing boxers with more Confederate bars and stars. They looked part Klan, part thug—and I'm not trying to say they weren't good, but they weren't great either.

Kirby claimed we had been robbed, that the judges were determined to let the one white team win. "What is this? Reverse affirmative action or something?" he yelled as we walked back to the car.

"Is that a thing?"

"Well, if white people can claim reverse racism, why can't we claim reverse affirmative action?"

I shrugged.

"They did a Macklemore/Kendrick Lamar on us, dude. Textbook okie doke."

We drove back across the Mississippi state line in complete silence, the radio off. I didn't know what to think of what happened. Were they really better than us? I tried to flip everything in my mind and see it the way the judges, a primarily black panel, would have seen it. Was it impressive that they were white and hanging in there? There had been white teams in the past, and this one—at least to me—didn't seem any more impressive than the others. These dudes had even ended their dap with the stereotypical high five.

Were they signifying with their handshake?

Could white people really signify?

Could black people continue to ignore the fact that we didn't really own anything anymore?

I still believed we were the better team. But I was biased, I knew.

With the blackness of the night washing through the car, blocking out our ability to see anything other than the highway centerline in front of us, I looked over at Kirby.

His gloves were balled up and pushed into the corner of the windshield, his hands elbow-deep in a bag of fried pork skins, his bug-eyed face black and blank.

Eight Million

The 2-Train. 5:30 p.m. Wall Street Station.

This packed box is a suffocating cloud of heat and breath.

I am stuck standing in front of an elderly West Indian woman, my junk only inches from her face, when the door opens, sucking in a new crowd of people and edging me over, giving her a mild reprieve. If we were not on wheels thundering through the bowels of The City, a fire marshal would have closed this space down by now. That's when I notice Janelle Simpson squeezing into the narrow space between me and a shaggy older white guy. She hasn't noticed me yet, but she will soon, because I will have to lift my arm to create space for her to grab the railing so that she doesn't fall.

As her hand eases beneath mine, our eyes connect. It's not so much recognition that I read as it is embarrassment. She probably thought that we'd never run into each other again. Not in this city of eight million people. Not on a train headed to Brooklyn (miles from our first date on the Upper West Side). I almost find myself smiling, because, like her, I had assumed that this situation would never happen.

But it has.

Now Janelle is literally trapped against me, her body filling in the space under my arm. The door closes, and the train begins to move, rocking her even farther beneath my arm so that her ass, voluptuous in her pantsuit, brushes slowly against my midsection.

I lean down and whisper into her ear, "Hello."

She turns to face me, her face crimson beneath her smooth brown skin, her glasses perched high atop her nose. She responds casually, "Hey."

The train charges through the tunnel, swaying her body back and forth against mine, and I remember *us*. It has been more than a year since I last saw her, yet I still remember the feel of her straddling me, her hips rotating aggressively. We couldn't get enough of each other that weekend, and in my delusion, I thought it was the beginning of something special, but then she disappeared--not a phone call, not a trace.

She probably never figured she'd see me again, yet here we are.

As the train continues to race along the rails, I swear I can feel her hips rotating against me, the movement distant, yet strangely familiar. I adjust myself so that I am rubbing against her, and we sway back and forth with the rhythm of the car.

She doesn't look back to acknowledge me, yet she continues to press herself into me, and I welcome her, afraid to admit to myself that I ever missed her.

As she leans her back into my chest, I notice people around, oblivious, stuffed into their own private miseries. We are invisible to them.

"Next stop Clark Street," the automated voice calls over the speaker.

As the car comes to a complete stop, Janelle slows her hips. I hold my breath, not wanting her to stop. Then I hear the automated voice again. I consider telling her that this is my stop, that we should exchange numbers and hook up again for old time's sake, but then I remember the anguish and embarrassment of leaving repeated messages on her voicemail only to realize that she would never call me back.

The door opens, and I quietly step back, easing out into a wave of people.

As the door closes, she turns to look for me. I can't make out her eyes behind her glasses at this distance, but I would like to believe that there is a pain in them, a pain that mirrors the pain I had in mine more than a year ago.

Eight million people, I tell myself, watching the train speed away.

Janelle, find me again, if you can.

Beat Bop

There are only two tragedies in life: one is not getting what one wants, and the other is getting it.

~ Oscar Wilde

So I'm showing my girlfriend the first page of my latest story when she tells me how it's not proper to start a sentence with a conjunction.

I can't tell if she's joking or not. Either way, it's hardly funny.

This conversation bores me, and it's only when I agree to accompany her to the Spitzer Museum downtown that she let's up and gives me space to breathe a little. There's an exhibit she wants to see by the latest in a line of up-and-coming street artists.

The subway ride feels longer than it really is. I listen to her tell me about how I need to be more cultured, how I need to elevate myself and embrace the arts. I tell her that she needs to elevate her taste in music. No grown woman should be choosing her musical selections from the radio.

We get off at our stop and walk three blocks to a nondescript building, take the elevator to the seventh floor, and step off into a large, partitioned loft. The recommended donation for entry is $15. I walk past the ticket counter. My girlfriend stays put, her purse tightly crossing her body.

"Excuse me, sir," a heavyset raven-haired woman says, pushing her glasses up the bridge of her nose. "It's $15 a piece."

"The sign says 'recommended,' not required."

"Sir," the woman repeats, "we're a nonprofit and donations are how we continue to operate."

My girlfriend looks embarrassed by this exchange and places her fists on her hips to emphasize her displeasure. I try to care, but it doesn't take.

"If you want everyone to pay, change the sign so it doesn't say 'donation.' And for god's sake, get rid of the word 'recommended.' *Required admission fee*. Hear that? See how it sounds different from *recommended donation*?"

"Sir?"

"Dammit, Ali! I'll pay for it then," my girlfriend says.

"Okay."

I can be such an asshole.

I know she will be angry with me for the rest of the day, but she won't be angry enough to end this sinking ship that we call a relationship. Not while she can claim a boyfriend when her so-called girlfriends can't.

I wait for her on the other side of the counter, and once she's paid, she walks past me, ignoring me.

"You okay?" I ask, catching up with her.

She continues to ignore me, so I give her space.

She heads toward a variety of exhibits along the side wall. I head in the opposite direction.

Most of what I see along the wall on the right and the partition that runs down through the center of the room is so abstract that I can't follow it. Some pictures are single, floating geometrical figures against solid colored backgrounds. Others look as if a dog ran through the studio knocking paint out of buckets and onto canvases. Not to belittle the artists in this museum, but I wonder if I could detonate a bag of paints over a canvas and get a few pieces accepted to this museum. The thought really sets in for a moment, as I consider people lining up to buy my prints, the artist grants that would roll in, and all of the women who would emerge from the woodworks to give my girlfriend a run for her money. I laugh when I realize I have been standing in the same spot for five minutes pondering this.

I look back to see if my girlfriend is nearby, but she has navigated the labyrinth of this large space and left me to my own devices. I consider seeking her out to apologize but change my mind. She's still heated. I'll give her a few more minutes to cool her heels. I'll offer to take her to her favorite sushi spot for dinner and smooth things over then.

Rounding one of the partitions, I find myself in a narrow corridor of paintings that dead-ends with a large portrait. On the placard next to the painting in a large, bold, italicized font is the word "Self-Portrait." I can read nothing else from this distance.

The woman in the painting is beautiful in a way that causes your face to twitch involuntarily. Her curly Afro radiates orange and yellow colors like the sun. She is naked down to her waist, which is as far as the painting goes. Her skin is like honey, a description that would normally horrify me, as it relates to food, an all too common African-American self-reference. Still, no other word comes to mind. Her eyes are painted so she appears to be looking directly at me. Her lips are full, tinted in a magenta—luscious, almost wet.

I stare at her, unable to look away. And then everything goes black.

"Ali, baby, are you okay?"

I hear my girlfriend's voice, but my eyes are apparently still closed.

"I'll call for an ambulance," I hear another voice say.

"Don't do that," I say, squinting, then opening my eyes.

"You passed out," my girlfriend says. "Let me call an ambulance."

"Don't do that. You know how much those things cost? My insurance is not that good," I joke.

The raven-haired woman with the glasses gives me a fake chuckle and backs away cautiously. Although people in this city are a litigious bunch, I have no plans of going to a hospital or trying to sue this place.

My girlfriend helps me to my feet, and as I stand, I turn and catch sight of the portrait on the back wall. My knees buckle for a moment, so I look away.

"You sure you're okay?"

I nod. "I'm cool. Must've locked my knees while I was standing here. I probably just need some air."

My girlfriend nods, takes my hand, and guides me out of the gallery and onto the elevator.

"Hey, I'm sorry about earlier," she says.

"*I'm* supposed to be the one apologizing."

"Let's just go back to my place. You can lie down, and I could rub your back," she offers.

Her concern touches me, and I feel ashamed of myself for the way I acted earlier. "I wanted to take you out to Wantanabe's this evening."

"We can do that tomorrow. Let's get you to bed now. It would make me feel more comfortable if you were resting since you don't want to go to a hospital."

I reluctantly agree. I had actually had my mouth set for some California rolls, but I give her the benefit of the doubt. I can't remember ever having fainted, and she might be right about my needing to get to a bed.

We take a taxi back to her building, and when we reach her apartment, she helps me to her room. I lie on the bed and she covers me with a lightweight comforter.

She then kisses my forehead, turns off the light, and returns to lie in the bed beside me.

I do not deserve this woman. I never have.

With the shades pulled tightly, the room ushers in the night immediately. I close my eyes, and as I feel her lay her head upon my chest, I remember the portrait of the woman in the gallery and an erection emerges, thick and powerful, unyielding and eager. I lean over in one fluid motion, edging my girlfriend from my chest and onto her back, where I begin kissing her passionately. For a moment she is startled, but she quickly acquiesces, tugging on my shirt so that it slides up my chest and over my head.

We don't speak; we only indulge in this extemporaneous moment, and while she rotates her body beneath mine, I keep my eyes closed, imaging the woman in the painting.

I wake in complete darkness and sit up in the bed, unable to see a centimeter in front of my face. I reach for my girlfriend and feel her warm naked back beneath my fingertips. I scoot slowly to the other side of the bed and swing my legs over the side, planting my bare feet against the cool hardwood floor. With my hands stretched in front of me, I feel for the chair that contains my draped clothes. For a moment I consider dressing and leaving but think against it. I have already played the bad guy once today.

Instead, I walk to the window of her bedroom and peak through the blinds into the city. It extends on for what looks like miles, street corner lights punctuating the end of one block and the beginning of another. The street is beautiful, still glistening from the rain that beat against the window sill earlier.

I turn around to face my girlfriend, the light behind me still piercing the blinds. She is asleep, blissfully unaware of the fact that I am unable to stop thinking about the woman in the painting.

My phone is in the case clipped to my jeans, so I walk over and take it out carefully, angling it so that the light of the screen will not awaken her. I google the Spitzer Museum, and once I have selected the website, I scan to the page that lists the current artists who have featured exhibits in the gallery. I am surprised at how thorough the website is. There are roughly forty artists listed with links to their own individual websites.

It was a self-portrait. That's what the placard next to the painting said. That means that there is a real woman out there who is the inspiration for the painting I saw. In that moment I wonder if looking up this artist will destroy my fantasy. Although the image in the portrait looked realistic, that did not necessarily mean that the painting is identical to image of the painter. Who knew what creative liberties had been taken? Still, if she captured herself on canvas at least as well as Frida Kahlo had done, that would be enough to sustain my interest. One could have easily looked at a Kahlo painting and then recognized her if she had walked into a room.

When I try to remember the name of the artist, I realize that I was never close enough to the painting to read anything other than its title. As I sit on the edge of the bed, I stare at the list of artist names. I immediately exclude the names that are masculine and begin the process of clicking the links of each of the feminine names. With each link I am guided to a personal website where I have to scan the pages looking for anything that resembles the style of the painting I saw.

I do this for an hour before I hear my girlfriend stir behind me.

"What are you doing?" she asks.

"Just checking my email," I say, locking my screen and placing my phone back in the clip.

"Come here."

I crawl back beneath the sheets, worried that she will read my mind. I don't know why this scares me when I often ponder my own apathy toward this relationship, but it does.

"Are you okay?" she asks.

"I'm fine."

"I'm going to have to take you to the museum more often."

I ease my back up onto my pillow. "What do you mean?"

"If you pass out and come to and stroke me like that, I'd say that's a trade-off worth considering." She chuckles, pleased with her joke.

I play along. "So you like how I stroke you?"

"It was different this time, though," she says, suddenly sounding serious.

"How so?"

"Not saying that you don't want me, but it seemed like you *really* wanted me this time."

If you only knew the half, I think.

Rather than respond, I nod and lean over, kissing her on the cheek.

"What was that for?"

"I just wanted to thank you."

She is content with this answer and nestles herself beneath my arm, resting her head on my chest.

She doesn't realize it, but she has confirmed my need to continue my search.

I leave my girlfriend's place as dawn breaks over the city. I tell her I have to get home because I have a few meetings this morning. She doesn't complain, as she has to report to her job at 9 a.m. She asks if she can see me later this evening, but I remain noncommittal, citing a magazine article I'm freelancing that is bumping against a deadline.

The subway ride across town is peaceful. I replay the last twenty-four hours, anxious to look at my phone and continue my research, but I have a rule about pulling out electronics on the train. Even in a city this beautiful, there is no absence of crime.

When I reach my apartment, I grab my laptop and toss myself across the bed. Within seconds, I have found my spot on the Spitzer Museum website, sorting through the various artists.

I make it through the feminine names to no avail. I then look at the remaining names. Several of them appear androgynous, so they are my second set of names to research.

Cameron. Aston. Brett. Coby. Daryl. Yannick.

And then Riley.

Riley Scott.

When I see the homepage, I feel as though someone has kicked all of the air out of my lungs. There are two portraits side by side: one is the beautiful naked woman I had seen in the museum, the one who gave me my first bout of Stendahl Syndrome ever; the other is a portrait of a man naked from the waist up. Even at a glance it is clear that the faces are identical, save for the hair and breasts. They are identified as "Self Portrait 1" and "Self Portrait 2."

I stare at both pictures, confused, my finger poised to click through the rest of the site for an explanation of what I am seeing, but I pass out again.

Stendahl Syndrome is the rare situation when a person is so overcome with emotion from looking at an artistic piece that he or she literally loses consciousness. There are similar conditions, like Paris Syndrome, a condition widely associated with Asians who have visited the Louvre and have become so overwhelmed with emotion at the sight of those masterpieces that they lose it. Then there is Jerusalem Syndrome, which overtakes people whose religious histories tie to the area. Needless to say, the Spitzer Museum is not a place for which any of these psychosomatic conditions would conceivably take place.

I come to, my head resting next to my laptop. My display is asleep, and when I awaken it, the twin images are facing me. I click on the "About" link on the toolbar to avoid drifting off again.

The bio is short:

Riley Scott is a native of Austin, Texas. She is a graduate of Spelman College, where she earned her BA in Art, and of Columbia University, where she earned an MFA in Visual Arts. She is the winner of a National Endowment for the Arts fellowship, and her work has been exhibited in several museums and galleries around the country and in France. She is currently living in The City, where she focuses primarily on oil-based paintings that explore the roles of gender and beauty in American society.

While her bio is impressive (not to mention short), I can't deny the sense of relief I feel when I realize Riley is indeed a woman. Still, the fact that she is also in The City allows for the possibility of our paths crossing.

I refocus my attention on clicking through the other links on her site. There are no actual photographs of her on her website, but a quick Google search of her images reveals pictures of her at various award banquets.

She looks exactly like her painting, and I feel my pulse quicken. I close my laptop and lie on my back, staring up at the ceiling, the white paint reflecting the morning sunshine over my room in a golden glow.

Riley Scott.

I spend the morning googling everything I can about Riley Scott. By lunchtime I have transformed myself from merely a fan into a "Stan."

The luxury of being a freelancer is that I don't have to report to an office. The flipside of that is that I have to work my ass off all of the time because of the erratic payment schedules and amounts. Each month I cobble together my existence a few checks at a time. Occasionally I get ahead with my finances, but most of the time I am struggling to keep up. So while I am happy I can fuck around on the Internet scanning articles on Riley Scott, I don't really have the time to spend on this type of activity.

Unless.

I pick up my cell phone and call Gladys Mathews over at *Belle Noire* magazine.

"Ali, what's up?"

"Gladys, I have an idea for an article I wanted to run by you."

Because my relationship with Gladys goes back seven years, she has allowed me to pitch her informally over the years. I waste no time pitching her on Riley Scott, emphasizing the womanist angle of her artwork. I then reference Renee Cox and Kara Walker, two artists who were featured in their magazine over the past year. After a few minutes, she agrees to have me email her something a bit more formal so she could run it by her editor-in-chief.

When I get off the phone, I put together the email and send it out. If they approve the article suggestion, I can afford to put more resources behind this thing. In the meantime I return to Riley's website and check her contact information. I don't see any information for an agent, so I imagine that she responds directly to inquiries herself.

I check my watch and see that it is 1:37 p.m., and this only makes me feel even more sluggish. I hop in the shower and get dressed. I have nowhere to go, but on a beautiful day like today, I don't want to waste it sitting in my apartment staring at a laptop. Plus, I need to clear my head.

Before yesterday I knew nothing about Riley Scott. Now I feel obsessed—and that's not a good thing. I swear to myself at that moment that I will chill on this obsession kick. It's not a good look for a brother in my position. I have a girlfriend, and I've never been known to be this thirsty for anything.

I lock the apartment door behind me, walk down the street, and lose myself in the wonders of the city.

Footsteps on concrete sound like percussion, and if you listen closely enough, you can hear your heartbeat syncopating with the pat-shuffle-pat of each person moving around you. The sounds of pigeons, taxi horns, and the rhythmic cadences of the people conversing are like music, as the sun pushes through the leafy limbs that canopy the sidewalks and children skip rope or hopscotch through colored chalk grids. June is alive, and we are breathing it.

With my earbuds resting in my ears, I walk nearly forty blocks, my mind moving fluidly through each song on my playlist. I try not to think about Riley and feel that I am successful until I realize I am trying not to think about her.

My phone rings, interrupting the song playing in my ears. I check the display. It's my girlfriend.

"Hey, you!" I say, answering the call.

"Whatchu doin'?"

"Walking around midtown, clearing my head to do some writing this evening. What's up?"

"Just thinking about last night and how good it was."

I smile but the guilt of my excessive fantasizing needles at me. "It *was* good," I offer.

"So can I see you tonight?"

It's an odd question. We've been together for a little over a year, and while it hasn't knocked either of us off our feet, we have hung tight, an investment we are both hoping will pay off. Still, to identify one night of great sex out of a year of sex would make me more suspicious than amorous.

"We can do that," I respond.

"Good. I'll cook dinner. Can you come through around seven?"

"I'll be there."

I hang up the phone, and the music starts back up, almost as if it had never stopped.

I met my girlfriend at the city park during a Roy Ayers concert. The morning rain had become the afternoon rain, and by the time Roy started his set, only the most loyal of fans were still braving the weather. Droplets fell from the sky in tablespoons, splattering across heads, faces, and shoulders. From where I stood Roy was hazy behind the sheet of water separating the audience from the stage.

"Searching" had the loyalists bobbing their heads, in spite of the rain, but as soon as the electric piano and xylophone from his classic song "Everybody Loves the Sunshine" started, something peculiar happened: the rain stopped and the sun emerged into the bright blue sky from behind the clouds. We reached our hands to the sky, almost like a spiritual ritual, and in that moment the music connected everyone in the audience together through a melodic thread and we were the fabric of something beyond beautiful.

It was then that I saw my girlfriend, her fingertips outstretched, the remains of the earlier shower dripping down her forearms and elbows. The sun kissing her brown skin was all I needed to see to guide my way through the throng of people filling the large space at the foot of the stage. My feet carried me before I became aware I was moving.

As soon as I reached her, I wanted to say something clever, but words failed me. She did notice me, though. Her smile may have been the result of the music blanketing us, or maybe she was welcoming me into her space.

"Hi. I'm Ali."

She continued smiling and offered me her name. At that moment I thought it was one of the most beautiful names I had ever heard, but as time passed I thought less and less of it, until finally I stopped using it altogether, preferring instead to call her "baby" or one of a number of pet names I yanked from the land of Generica.

But at that moment she could have tied me into a square knot around her finger. When the concert ended, we continued our conversation over fried plantains and coco bread. Things escalated from there.

Initially art was one of the things that bonded us. She was very much into the fine arts, and much of that rubbed off on me; I was very much into music, and much of that rubbed off on her. The irony is that, even now, we have arguments about how "uncultured" the other is when it comes to our artistic passions. In that regard we are both full of shit, and while it seems like we would have the makings of longevity, given how we met, I have become increasingly more bored with our relationship. I am not alone in this assessment either. Her complaints about how predictable I am are at an all-time high, and even our arguments have become predictable—which should, in theory, prevent us from having them as often as we do.

I think we have both been hanging around, hoping that something would happen to jumpstart the magic again. I sense that she views last night as a possible catalyst for this spark. The only problem is that I didn't bump my head and fall in love with her all over again; I bumped my head and fell completely out of love with her.

I catch the train down to the southern tip of the city, getting off at a park that faces the river. This is my favorite place to go because it reminds me of home, a peninsula city on the coast of Virginia. I grew up around water and plan to die around water. There is simply a tranquility that comes from staring out at the water as it rolls back and forth, full, abyss-like, endless.

I find a bench facing the river and watch the water glisten beneath an auburn sky. I want to give my girlfriend the benefit of the doubt that we are breaking new ground, and I allow myself to dwell on her, to fantasize about those moments where I truly felt the passion of our connection. Maybe I could rededicate myself to this relationship and become a better boyfriend. Last night was good, even if I had someone else on my mind. But when you think about it, how many relationships have *really* been salvaged by the unknown presence of an outside person?

No relationship is ever completely bad. There are moments when things are amazing. The problem is people get tired of chasing a high that can never come again. I remember nights when my girlfriend and I made love, the cool fall air seeping in from the open window, Eric Benet playing softly in the background as I explored her femininity. I can remember nights when we made love while listening to *Maxwell's Urban Hang Suite* over and over, taking the time to enjoy our own moans during the six minute break of the last track. Yes, we definitely had some moments, and if life were only a series of moments with nothing in between, that would be more than enough for me. But at this point in my life, the bridges and transitions count for a lot more.

Not that any other woman would necessarily offer me anything different from my girlfriend; still, it doesn't stop me from wondering if one could.

Maybe that's what scares me about Riley Scott—or what she represents: the possibility of something better.

On the way back to my apartment, I hear back from Gladys Mathews. She gives me the green light to write five hundred words on Riley Scott. And just like that Riley is square in the center of my thoughts again.

Even more, I now have the weight of *Belle Noire's* media influence, which should make getting to Riley a bit easier.

When I reach my apartment, I decide to forgo further research for my article and instead prepare to head over to my girlfriend's place. I dock my phone in the speakers by the sink in my bathroom and turn on some music. The clock reads 5:45.

I toss my clothes into the hamper and hop in the shower. With the heat of the water blasting against my back, I lower my head, facing the showerhead so the water runs down my scalp and across my face. I open my mouth and inhale the steamy air, remembering times when I made love to my girlfriend in this very spot, our bodies meshing in the moistness of this cloud.

I feel fingers stroking my back and reaching around to touch my chest. The caress is soft and my skin tingles. I place my hands on the wall in front of me, leaning forward, and I feel her resting her chest upon my back, her arms wrapping around me.

Nothing in this surprises me until I look down and see her hands. They are not those of my girlfriend; their honey-tinted hue causes me to stand more erect. I turn around slowly, my eyes large with wonder.

I start to say her name, but she places her finger to my lips, silencing me. Her curly Afro glows in the light of dusk, water dripping loosely from her hair. I stare, taking in her body. Each curve takes me back to the painting at the Spitzer. She smiles at me and slides her warm, wet hands along the sides of my face, pulling me closer. Her lips taste like oranges when she kisses me deeply.

The steam in the shower blinds my vision, and I am only able to see her and nothing else. She eases her body up close to mine, and we embrace, perspiration and steam intermingling so that we create our own storm. I have never been more aroused, and she feels this, as she takes me in her hands.

She smiles knowingly.

I reach back for the wall, to steady myself, but nothing is there. Only the cloud around us.

She places her hands on my shoulders and lifts her legs one at a time. I take her frame in my hands, helping to support her. Straddling my waist, she reaches down and guides me into her. The heat of her body envelops me, and my flesh begins to glow, an orange tint radiating just above my skin. She is glowing as she moves her body up and down, the mist between us illuminated by our ecstasy.

We are the sun.

I close my eyes, allowing every cell in my body to indulge in this tingling sensation. Then I open them.

I am alone, and the water has grown lukewarm, the temperature falling by the second. I have no idea of how long I have been standing here, but I look at the clock on the wall of the bathroom, and it reads 6:30. I jump from the shower and start drying myself. I can already tell I will be late.

As I dress I still feel my skin tingling, as if it is remembering the kiss of the sun.

I leave the apartment just before 7 and call my girlfriend to let her know I'm running late but I'm on the way.

"No problem," she responds.

"Why are you sweating?" my girlfriend asks, while I sit across from her looking at the skinless chicken breast adorned in thin slices of orange.

"It's warm in here."

"I'm sorry," she responds. "I can turn the temperature down."

"Don't worry. I can open a window. You've done enough," I say. "This dinner looks amazing!"

"I can't wait for you to try it."

I stand and slide open the window nearest me and return to my seat at the table. I take my knife and fork and cut a piece of the chicken. When I taste it, I smile.

"You like it?"

I nod. "It's delicious."

She begins eating, and I think to myself that this is not so bad after all. We haven't had a night like this in quite some time.

We sit, eating in silence, until my girlfriend says, "I picked you up a gift."

"You didn't have to do that. I came here empty-handed."

"It's not about that. I just saw something that I thought you might like."

"Well, okay then."

She rises from the table and walks into her bedroom, only to return with a cardboard tube.

In the year that we have been together, she has given me two other gifts that came in cardboard tubes, both of which are hanging in the den of my apartment. She is insistent on helping me to grow my art collection, one print or lithograph at a time.

"You didn't have to do this," I say kindly, but I mean it.

She chuckles. "But I wanted to. This is a piece that I think you should have. It's only a print, but it's been signed."

"Thank you, baby," I respond. "I'll take a look at it after dinner."

"No. I want you to open it now."

I point my fork at the chicken. "But this is so good."

"Please," she responds. I know she cherishes the expression on my face when I see one of the prints she has selected for me, so I yield to her.

I take the cardboard tube from her and twist off the top. I tilt the tube and the print, wrapped in light tissue paper, slides out slowly. I remove the length of the rolled print from the tube.

"This is an artist to watch," she says. "She's at the beginning of an amazing career."

She? My pulse quickens and I can feel my hands perspiring. I place the print across my lap and wipe my hands on my slacks to dry them.

"She is featured at the Spitzer," my girlfriend adds.

As I slowly unroll the print, I see the honey-like hue of a naked stomach. I know this painting like I do my own phone number. I stop unrolling it and look up. "Thank you, baby. This is really nice of you."

"But you haven't unrolled it yet."

"I don't want to get it dirty. I haven't washed my hands yet."

"Come on," she says, removing the print from my lap in one smooth movement. She unrolls it so quickly that I can't look away.

I feel my legs weaken, and all I can think to do is soften my gaze until my eyes are completely unfocused. I nod enthusiastically, trying to maintain my composure. "Thank you. It's a great piece."

I take the piece from her, keeping my eyes on her, while I roll the print back up.

"Are you sure you like it? You didn't really get a good look at it."

"Trust me. I saw it and I love it." I place the print back in the tube. "Just curious, but what is it about this print that made you buy this for me?"

"Riley Scott is one of the hottest new artists around. She's still largely unknown, but it's only a matter of time before she breaks through. Plus, I saw you looking at this painting at the gallery. I thought that maybe you liked it."

"Well, thank you," I respond. Up until this moment I didn't know that my girlfriend had witnessed what had happened. The fact that she saw everything and didn't make the connection between my fainting and Riley

Scott's painting is a testament to my girlfriend's desire to see only what she wants to see.

"I have one more thing for you," she says, rising from her seat.

"Please, baby," I say. "You've done enough."

"I'll be right back," she responds, ignoring me.

When she leaves the room this time, I am alone with the Riley Scott print lying across my lap. The fabric of my pants feels as though it will burst from my erection. Still, I am eager to unroll the print and get one good look at it, to take in Riley's naked beauty once more and allow that feeling to settle over me and give me a comfort I can't get from anywhere else.

"Ta-da," my girlfriend says, emerging from her bedroom, dressed in a black negligee. "It's time for dessert."

I fly into her arms immediately.

In the lucidity of post-orgasmic bliss, I realize that Riley Scott—or her likeness—is both helping my relationship with my girlfriend and simultaneously hurting it. The reinvigoration of our sex life is a breath of fresh air and hints at the promise of longevity in a relationship that was only days ago flailing like a headless chicken running around a farm. But our relationship, as it is now, reminds me more of that famous headless chicken named Mike who toured the world during the 1940s. It apparently still has some life left in it. The bad part is that what we have is dependent on someone else.

I think about this as I lie in bed next to my girlfriend. It feels like a repeat of last night, and it begins to dawn on me that we have now initiated a pattern. I can't afford to do this another night. It just doesn't seem fair.

I laugh at this thought. I'm apparently not a 100% asshole after all.

"What are you thinking?" my girlfriend asks.

"Nothing. I'm just chillin'. What about you?"

"Our future."

"What about it?"

"You know. Stuff."

I shift uncomfortably. "What kind of stuff?"

She sits up and turns on the lamp by her bed. "Have you thought about where we're going with this relationship?"

Kid gloves, I remind myself.

"Well, we've been together for a year, so that means we're getting to know each other a lot better."

I'm hoping that my qualifying the length of our relationship might push back some of the speculation about our future, at least for the time being.

"But where do you see us going with our relationship?" she asks.

"Where do *you* see us going with our relationship?"

"I asked you first."

"But you're the one who brought up this topic."

We sound like children, and the conversation is already beginning to disgust me. I take a deep breath and answer when she remains silent. "Let's just see where things go."

"Humph," she says, crossing her arms, clearly not satisfied with my comment.

"I take it I didn't say the right thing," I say.

"There is no right thing to say."

We sit up in the bed, silent and not really looking at each other. After such intense intimacy earlier, the awkwardness of the situation is heightened.

"Can I ask you a question?" she finally asks.

"Sure," I say reluctantly.

"Do you love me?"

"Yeah."

"I mean, are you *in* love with me?"

I hesitate a second too long, and all hell breaks loose.

The tears fall as if she has held her face to a thunderstorm. I move to comfort her, but she nudges me away.

"I think you should leave," she says through clenched teeth.

I try to hug her again, but to no avail. "What did I do?"

"I can't even talk about it right now," she says, wiping her eyes. "You should leave."

"So you're kicking me out of your crib? Are you serious? It's like two o'clock in the morning—and it's cold out there."

She turns her back to me as she sits on the edge of the bed. For the life of me I can't tell what I did that set her off, but there is a small voice buried in the back of my head that is whispering, "Isn't this what you wanted, Ali? Just leave."

I stand and grab my clothes. "If I leave, I won't be coming back."

My threat is idle, and she knows this. Still, she responds, "I'm not kicking you out. I just need some space, and this apartment is too small for that."

I pull my shirt over my shoulders. "I'm going to wind up sitting in the train station for half an hour waiting for one to come at this time of night."

"I can give you money for a cab," she says.

When she says that, I snap. "Fuck it. I'm out of here."

"So you're gonna go *there*? Cursing me out?"

"I didn't say 'fuck *you*.' I said, 'fuck *it*.'" I shake my head, frustrated beyond words. "Don't worry. I'll let myself out."

She doesn't move from the edge of the bed, so I leave the bedroom and head for the front door, stopping only to grab my print.

With Riley tucked under my arm, the argument with my girlfriend is already starting to become a faint memory as I walk down the street.

I spend the following morning staring at the print until I can look at it without my heart rate accelerating.

This takes about two hours. It feels almost like hearing a hilarious joke and being forced to listen to it until it no longer elicits even a smile.

Occasionally I stare at my cellphone, half-expecting to see the display come to life with a text message or phone call from my girlfriend. When it doesn't, I contemplate if I should call her and make some effort to smooth things over. But then I remember the cool walk to the train station and my struggle to stay awake while the train took its sweet time coming. I still can't believe that she kicked me out of her place. That only works on a sit-com. In the real world kicking someone out of a house is one of the most deliberately disrespectful things you can do to that person, second only to spitting in his or her face. I'm not saying that there may never come a need to do either of those things, but I definitely don't think that last night's events merited that kind of stinging, unforgettable diss.

So, no, I won't be calling her.

I can be a bigger man, but not a giant.

Instead, I am pulling together research for my article and preparing to draft an email to Riley, asking if I can interview her for *Belle Noire*. Because of the way Riley's website is set up, I will try first to contact her using the method she requested there, which is essentially to use her direct email address.

I open up one of her pictures on Google Images and stare at it for a moment. She is so beautiful that it angers me, because if I were unable to be with her, I would know that she was always out there in the world, making whoever I did end up with a clear second choice.

There are pictures of her receiving awards, her curly hair a sphere of soul and hip-hop rolled into one; there are also pictures of her painting in her studio, dressed only in a sleeveless brown ribbed t-shirt and a pair of navy blue Spelman sweatpants, her hair pulled back into a bun. I can scarcely make out a tattoo of scripted words running along her inner right arm, but the shot isn't tight enough for me to read the words.

In one black and white photograph she is leaning against a mural that she painted of The City's nighttime skyline, stars in the sky mirroring the glow of office lights in the skyscrapers. She is wearing a dark colored baby t-shirt that reads "Got Soul?" and a pair of denim fitted capri pants, her very shapely calves exposed, her feet beautifully pedicured in a pair of open-toed heels. This is the picture I look at that longest. I trace every detail, imagining what it would be like to be in her presence, and the thought both thrills *and* chills me.

If I passed out just from looking at her painting and have whipped myself into a nervous frenzy from just looking at her photographs, then what would happen if I were to actually meet her? This thought arises swiftly and, like a damp blanket, threatens to choke out the fire of my longing.

I close my laptop. I clearly need to get a handle on myself. My fear is not just irrational; it's unprofessional.

My girlfriend minored in art history when she was in college as a way of compromising with her parents, who wanted her to focus all of her attention on a major in business. She admitted to me that her master plan was to combine both art and business and become an art buyer, just like Whitley Gilbert from the television show *A Different World*. For one reason or another, the dream didn't materialize after college, and she found herself getting a job in marketing, where she has remained ever since. The only usage she has gotten from her art history minor is what she has shared with me—and whoever came before me.

At first the fact that she was an art lover from corporate America and I was a writer who freelanced primarily for music publications was enough to keep things interesting. We treated it like the first half of *Love Jones*, falling all over each other and playing the roles of buppie-bohos who only needed a Dionne Farris soundtrack to jumpstart our impromptu lovemaking sessions. Then she asked me how I felt about our moving in together. I hesitated and things went south from there. That was our biggest fight up until that point, and it took us a while to get past it. Things just weren't the same after that. I had been put to the test, in her eyes, and shown her that I wasn't ready for a commitment.

Given her kicking me out of her apartment last night, I would say that my hesitations have been at the heart of every major problem we have endured this far. But this time around I have neither the inclination nor the energy to fix things. The way I see it, we can't have a lasting relationship if she won't give me a moment to consider her questions in earnest. I'm sure if someone asked for her side of things, it would be quite different, though. Either way, I am not convinced that we are right for each other—and that's a bad space to be in when I have these thoughts about Riley Scott dancing through my thoughts.

My email to Riley is short and to the point. I introduce myself and tell her about the piece I'm doing for *Belle Noire*. I then ask if I might be able to interview her regarding the article and close out by providing her with my contact information. Now all I have to do is wait for her response.

If I ever needed a calling card to get to anyone, my journalism credentials have always worked. As a result, I am not worried about whether or not I will meet Riley, nor am I worried about how to conduct this interview. I have been freelancing for a while, and this is how I make my living.

I am, however, concerned about the memorability of my impression upon her, if in fact there is actually room to make an impression. If she is not interested, yes, it will sting, but I would have no intention of continuing my pursuit. The rejection from unrequited interest is often its own repellent.

To keep my mind off waiting for Riley's reply, I open my laptop and check my work calendar for this week's deadlines. I have two record reviews, neither more than 250 words. I have already listened to both LPs repeatedly and jotted my notes into separate Word documents. Now all I have to do is type each draft, do edits, and email them to *Midnight Jukebox* and *Thunderbox* magazines. Next week's schedule is a bit more involved, but at least I have gotten much of the heavier research out of the way already; in fact, I am often ahead of schedule, which is one of the reasons I have been able to last in this career as long as I have.

I pull up the LP I am reviewing for *Midnight Jukebox* on my cellphone and dock it on the speakers situated atop my desk. I bang out the rough draft of the review, while listening to the music. This allows me to add some last minute thoughts into the draft, ones that escaped my initial impressions. After I finish, I head to the kitchen and make a fruit smoothie for lunch, down it, and return to my room to take an early afternoon siesta. When I awake, I do some stretches and light exercises before sitting at my desk again and doing the editing portion of the first review. Within the hour, I have emailed my review to Scott Ericsson, the music editor at *Midnight Jukebox*, and am gearing up to work on my *Thunderbox* review.

My window is open so that the sounds of the street pour into the room: cars driving by, the percussive sounds of neighborhood vernacular, and other random sounds ranging from a creaky bicycle to what sounds like a bus door opening and closing. The air is brisk, but the sky is clear and bright. I look at the time on my cell phone and contemplate catching the train down to one of the piers and gazing out at the water that lines either side of The City's peninsula. Instead, I change out my playlist and pull up the notes for my next review.

Just as I am completing the first draft, the music coming from my phone stops in mid-song. I glance at the display and see the word "Unknown" flash across the screen as the phone rings.

I lift it from the dock, pressing the answer button. "Hello?"

"Hello. May I speak to Ali Shepherd?"

"This is he."

"My name is Riley Scott, and I'm following up on an email you sent earlier today."

The surprise of her call nearly knocks me out of my chair. Her firm alto voice throws me for a loop because I had expected it to be lighter and higher, like Minnie Riperton's. Instead it sounds more like Mary J. Blige's, a raw sexiness with a street edge.

"I wasn't expecting you to follow up so soon. I'm used to waiting at least a day before hearing back from someone."

"Well, do you want me to call back tomorrow?"

"No, this is a good time."

"Okay. I have to say I was pretty ecstatic about your email. I'm a fan of *Belle Noire*."

"That's good to hear," I say. "I caught your exhibit down at the Spitzer and pitched the idea to an editor over there who is a good friend of mine."

"Nice. So did you like the exhibit?"

I know what I want to say, but I can't fix my mouth to actually get out the words. Instead, I cough and clear my throat. "Hold on a sec."

"No problem," she says.

I mute the phone, sit it on my desk, and shake my hands like they're wet and I'm trying to dry them. All the while I am breathing as deeply as I can to calm my nerves. I sit back down and grab the phone, unmuting it.

"I thought it was amazing," I finally respond.

She laughs. "I'm glad to hear you say that. In this business you can never tell how people feel about what you're doing. One time an art critic cozied up to me at a gallery only to slam me in his column a few days later. I learned you can't assume anything, so I'm in the business of not taking anything for granted."

"You don't have to worry. I'm not writing about you to slam you. In fact, I guess you could call me a fan."

She sighs with relief. "Well, that's a good thing."

I chuckle. "You're in good hands."

"Cool. Well, feel free to start whenever you're ready."

"Huh?"

"With your questions."

It's only in this moment that I realize she expects me to conduct the interview over the phone. I'm embarrassed that I never considered the possibility she would actually expect me to do the interview this way. In my mind, I had imagined her emailing me back, and I would have then scheduled for us to meet somewhere quaint, like a neighborhood coffee shop, and do the interview there. Afterwards, we would continue talking, and I would offer to take her out to dinner, if she were interested. Yep. I had all of these grand notions and not a single one of them included the present scenario I am now experiencing.

Once I'm able to get past my faux pas, I say, "If you don't mind, maybe we could meet in person to do the interview. That way I can get a few pictures to accompany the article."

"Whatever works for you is good for me," she says. "So when and where? I'm pretty flexible in the mornings—if that's an option."

"The mornings are fine. Is there a place you'd prefer to do the interview?"

"Just come by my studio. It's on 208 Nina Simone Place, over in Berry Hill."

"Cool. Say ten a.m.?"

"That'll work. See you then."

When I hang up the phone, I feel myself smiling so hard my face is beginning to hurt.

I awaken with the sound of the doorbell. I didn't even realize I was asleep.

The clock on my wall reads a little after eleven p.m.

I stumble to the door in the clothes I have been sleeping in for the past few hours, wondering who in the hell it could be at my door this late at night. I grab the aluminum baseball bat I have next to the door and lean in to check the peephole.

It's my girlfriend.

"Give me a second," I call out, as I put the bat down.

I open the door and she walks in, her trench coat tied tightly around her waist.

"Did I catch you at a bad time?" she asks.

I rub the sleep from my eyes. "I just woke up. I must have fallen asleep earlier."

"I just wanted to say that I'm sorry about last night."

"Yeah. Okay," I say, wondering if I should return the favor of kicking her out of my place. "You could have just called me. You didn't have to come all the way over here, especially at this time of night."

"I had to see you," she says. "Do you forgive me?"

"I guess so," I say, wanting more than anything for her to leave.

"Don't be like that, Ali."

"Like what?"

She runs her hand down my chest. "Smile for me."

I muster enough energy for my cheeks to rise.

"That's good," she says. "Be a good boy, and I'll give you your gift."

Another gift? I muse, as she opens her coat to reveal her nakedness.

I hold my smile in place and allow her apology to proceed uninterrupted.

The sunlight streams through the blinds in my bedroom, and I open my eyes. I strain to see the clock on my wall. Nine o'clock. I stand up and take in the rumpled sheets. I can hardly remember anything that happened with my girlfriend last night. She had come with the trench coat doing the Robin Givens act from *Boomerang.* That much I remember.

Berry Hill is at least a twenty-five minute train ride from my part of the city, and because I'm already running behind, I grab a pair of jeans and a button-up from the hanger in my closet.

"What's the rush?" I hear coming from the doorway of the room. I jump, startled. When I see my girlfriend standing there in the doorway, wearing only a t-shirt from my drawer, a mug of coffee in each hand, I want to slap my face. I had no idea she was still here.

"Hey, you!" I say, clearly uncomfortable. I glance at the clock and the second hand is still ticking.

"I already called in sick for the day, so I'm yours."

"Oh," I chuckle uncomfortably, holding the shirt in my hand.

"Were you going somewhere?" she asks. "I can be ready in a few minutes."

This is incredibly awkward, and I kick myself for allowing myself to get into a situation like this when it now seems to have been so avoidable.

"Baby, I have to go do an interview for work, and I have to be there by ten."

"How long do you think it'll take?"

"I don't know. A few hours, I guess."

She nods, but I can see the disappointment on her face. "Can we at least do lunch and spend the afternoon together?"

I shrug my shoulders. "I don't know. I can call you when I finish, and we can go from there."

I can tell she doesn't like my answer, but she nods her agreement anyway. "Well, I guess I should get dressed so I can leave, too."

The tone in her voice suggests that she wants me to tell her she can stay in my apartment and wait for me, but that is not going to happen.

"I guess so."

I place my clothes on the bed and head toward the shower.

"Want company?" she asks.

I feel like I owe her for disrupting her morning, so I nod my head. "I still need to be out of here in ten minutes, though."

She smiles and removes her shirt. Her body looks nice in the morning light, and if I had more time, I would definitely give it a go.

With the hot water blasting my chest, she washes my back. I return the favor, washing her backside. When I turn to face her, she says, "So who are you interviewing?"

The question catches me off guard, and I find myself mumbling the answer.

"Who?"

"Riley Scott," I say.

"The painter? The one I bought you the print of?"

"Yeah. That's the one."

"You're interviewing her?"

"Yeah. I'm doing an article for *Belle Noire*."

She grabs a towel and starts drying herself. "Well, I guess you should get ready then."

I can't tell if she is bothered by any of this, but I don't have time to worry about it.

We dress quickly and I escort her to a cab. "I'll call you later," I say.

"Okay," she responds.

I lean over to kiss her, but she ducks into the cab and away from me. She doesn't look back as the cab pulls off.

As soon as her cab has turned the corner, I hail another one. When the driver pulls up to the curb, I say, "Nina Simone in Berry Hill. I need to be there in fifteen minutes."

"No problem," the guy responds, accelerating before I have even clasped my seatbelt.

True to his word, the driver pulls me up to the curb outside of Riley's studio at exactly ten. My mind is still racing, and I am starting to feel bad at the way things went down with my girlfriend. It feels like one step forward, two steps back. Maybe this is a sign that we should just end it.

I tip the driver, grab my messenger bag, and walk up to the door. 208 Nina Simone. I ring the buzzer. I can hear the sound echoing from behind the door.

The building that houses her duplex is old, like most of the other buildings in this part of town. The reddish bricks give it a quaint feel, though.

"Yes?" I hear Riley say via the intercom.

"This is Ali Shepherd."

The door buzzes, unlocking, and I walk in.

There is another set of doors in front of the entrance, and I stand here patiently awaiting her to unlock them.

When the door unlocks and opens, I see Riley standing in front of me in a ribbed sleeveless t-shirt and a pair of loose carpenter pants cuffed to her knees like capris. There are random paint droplets across her clothes, and she is wearing a pair of Keds that at one time had been white. Her hair is pulled back into a curly Afro puff and she is wearing a pair of thin-framed glasses. And her skin—the golden tint of it glows in the sunlight that drifts in from the doorway.

"Nice to meet you," she says, extending her hand.

I take hold of it, enjoying the warmth of her flesh pressed against mine. "The pleasure is all mine."

My legs weaken and I know that I am dangerously close to passing out. I will myself to hold it together, to make it through to the end of the interview.

"Wanna see the studio?" she asks.

"Sure."

I follow her through the building and we take a turn at the back wall and descend the stairs into her basement.

When my eyes take in the canvases lining the wall and the easels positioned around the room, I have to begin focusing on my breathing. The air feels thinner, like I have climbed to a higher altitude. It feels like I have entered one of her paintings.

Colors seem to swim around me: blues, pinks, reds, greens, browns, and yellows. The golden yellow colors bathe the room in a warm glow. Specks of paint decorate a large tarp-like mat that covers most of the floor in the studio.

"I have some chairs over here," she says, pointing to two folding chairs at the corner of the mat. "We can do the interview here."

She takes a seat, and I follow suit, taking out my phone and pulling up my voice recording app. I watch her as she crosses her legs and leans back in her chair. She is beautiful in a way that is both surreal, yet tangible.

"So are we ready to start?" she asks, snapping me from my staring. She smiles knowingly, and I wonder if am as transparent as I feel.

"Yeah. Okay. Let's get to it." I hold the phone between us. "How did you get started painting?"

She rubs her hands together, and I notice that she has several intricately designed rings that look as though they were handcrafted. Her hands are delicate and the silvery metal that wraps around them is both polished, yet sturdy.

"I actually didn't start painting until I turned sixteen. I remember my dad taking me to an exhibit by Jacob Lawrence at Hampton University's museum and thinking how Lawrence was able to convey such powerful stories through the simplicity of lines and shapes and color. Then we made it to another part of the museum where I saw Henry Tanner's *The Banjo Lesson*, alongside its counterpart, *The Bagpipe Lesson*, and I knew at that moment that I really wanted to paint. Up until then, I had only sketched in notebooks—nothing serious. But there I was, staring at these oil paintings with deep, rich hues, and I knew that I wanted to bring my drawings to life."

I nod encouragingly. "And you went to Spelman to study art?"

"Yeah. I was already headed there anywhere, since my parents had made that Morehouse/Spelman connection, but it worked out that Spelman had a strong art program."

"Did you think at that time you would be able to make a living from art?"

She smiles. "I don't think there's a way that any artist can predict whether or not she will be able to make a living from doing this. Many of us teach. Others work for ad agencies or pick up work as graphic designers. But deep down we each hope that maybe we could have our work featured in a gallery and maybe sell some art in the process."

"Well," I say, "I noticed that your Spitzer exhibit is amazing. Your self-portrait, in particular, is amazing."

"Thank you," she responds, "but which one are you referring to?"

"The one of you."

"They're both of me," she says, and it is only then that my mind races back to the dual female/male self-portraits featured on her website. In my bout of Stendahl I failed to notice the corresponding self-portrait at the Spitzer, which was probably somewhere in the vicinity of the other portrait.

"Oh. I meant the one of you as a female."

She laughs. "I'm just playing with you. I knew which one you meant."

I chuckle uncomfortably. "Why did you choose to paint yourself as a man?"

While I believe I have an idea of what her response will be, I am still hesitant. It is at this point that I question whether or not she is exactly who or what I think she is. Is is possible she could have attended Spelman as a transgender woman? I have to hold my mind in check as I await her response.

"I've always been fascinated with the intersection of gender roles and beauty in our society. For example, we say that women are pretty or beautiful, but we're hesitant to say a man is pretty unless we are mocking him or insulting him for his lack of overt machismo. We call men handsome, but why wouldn't we use the same word with women?" Her hands are moving as she says this. "I'm not the first artist to experiment with portraying herself in a different gender to examine societal parameters of beauty. While there is a heated debate over whether DaVinci painted himself in drag with the Mona Lisa, one thing you can't really ignore is that he used the spacial dimensions of his own face in painting her. The distance between each eye, the eyes and nose, the nose and mouth, all his."

"Interesting," I say. "What do you hope a viewer of your paintings will walk away with once they have seen them?"

"I would hope that they would ask themselves what qualifies as beauty in a society full of double standards, sexism, racism, and the objectification of the female body. We are so much more than our bodies," she says. "That's why I don't mind painting myself in the nude, because I know that is not the total of who I am."

I swallow, nodding my head. Have I been objectifying her? Where exactly is the line between admiration and objectification?

"Well," I say, composing myself, "your beauty comes through…" I feel myself sliding out of my chair and onto the mat, as the colors in the room come to life behind her and swallow me whole.

"Can you hear me?" I hear her say.

My mind is swimming, but I can scarcely make out the sound of Riley's voice inches above my face.

I open my eyes and the colors are still there, but this time they're static and not swimming. My forehead is cool, and my feet are propped up on a chair, more than likely the one I occupied before I passed out. I reach to touch my face, and Riley says, "I put a cool face cloth on your forehead. Are you okay?"

"Yeah," I say, embarrassed. I struggle to lower my feet from the chair, and she ends up having to help me get them down.

"You passed out," she says, as if I don't understand what happened. "They used to tell us in Phys Ed, 'If he's pale, raise his tail; if he's red, raise his head.' You were pretty pale."

I struggle to my feet and nearly fall.

"Be careful, man." She grabs my arm and assists me back to my chair. "I can call an ambulance if you want," she offers.

"Naw. I'm cool."

She stands in front of me, holding the damp cloth to my forehead. "We can finish this interview another day. You should probably lie down for a while."

"Seriously, I'm cool. I'd like for us to finish the interview, if that's all right with you."

She shrugs her shoulders. "If you're good, I'm good."

"Cool," I say, scanning the floor for my cell phone. It's lying next to my chair, so I reach over and pick it up. "Okay, where were we?"

"Are you sure about this?" Riley repeats.

"Definitely," I say, trying to sound unfazed. "I think I was asking you about the meaning of your paintings."

She nods. "I was telling you that I like to force my audience to explore the intersection of gender roles in our society."

"Yeah," I respond. "That sounds about right."

"You want some water?" she asks.

I realize now that she will not feel comfortable with me continuing the interview unless she can help me in some way, so I accept her offer.

"I'll be right back," she says, rising to her feet and heading for the stairs that lead back to the first floor. I watch, breath suspended, as she walks away, her natural gait smooth and sexy, even beneath her loose fitting pants.

I slowly stand and walk to the center of the paint-splattered mat on the floor. I am in the center of the room, and her art surrounds me. I will myself to stay on my feet while I move my eyes carefully from canvas to canvas. In nearly all of her paintings there is a depiction of her, some nude, some clothed, some female, some male—but it is all her. My eyes are more readily drawn to the nude female self-portraits, and my mind goes back to what she said earlier. Even with the knowledge of what she is attempting to do with her art, I can't deny how arousing her artwork is. As I stare at one lengthwise painting of her completely nude, her hands resting at her sides, I begin to question if I am actually objectifying her or if I am merely appreciating her beauty. At this point I can no longer tell. Maybe that's the point, though.

I hear her descending the stairs and cast my gaze toward her as she crosses the threshold.

"You probably shouldn't be standing," she says, offering me a glass of water.

"It's all right. I'm okay now."

She smiles and something in me ignites deep from within.

"I see that you are the sole subject in all of the paintings here. Is there any particular reason for that?"

She shrugs her shoulders. "I don't know. Why does any poet write about her life or any writer address the matters that pertain so deeply to her inner self? I guess it's the need to own yourself in your art and not hide behind it."

I nod. "And painting yourself in the nude? Is that a part of the idea of owning your art?"

"To be naked is to be perceived as vulnerable in this society," she says. "But you actually become invulnerable when you embrace your vulnerability. I have taken the power away from others by appropriating my body as art, rather than allowing others to objectify it against my will."

I take a closer look at the painting I was admiring before she returned to the room. "How would you know if you were being objectified or not? I mean, I am looking at this picture, but you can't read my mind."

She smiles. "I am not objectified because I am determining what and how you see me."

I take a sip of water and consider this. My personal curiosities are percolating, but I remind myself that I am here in a professional capacity and need to focus strictly on what I need for my article. "Well, I think your work speaks volumes."

She places a hand on her hip and looks directly into my eyes. "What about this painting speaks to you?"

I chuckle uncomfortably. "I don't know. You, I guess."

"You guess?"

"Well, no. I mean, yes. You are breathtakingly beautiful." This is my first candid admission since I arrived, and there's something liberating about getting this much out into the open.

"Thank you."

For a moment neither of us says anything, and I can't tell what I should say next. She looks at me with a patience on her face that suggests that she will wait until I speak again.

"Well, you told me how you became interested in art. Do you have any favorite artists?"

"Sure," she says. "Renee Cox is amazing, and she uses herself as a principal model for her photography. Frida is another one. But the person who has had the single biggest impact on my art is Jean-Michel Basquiat."

I think back to my earlier thoughts about the Basquiat wannabes I envisioned seeing at the Spitzer when my girlfriend initially dragged me there. I am both surprised and unsurprised by her response, although I don't put her in the class of wannabes at all.

"What is it about Basquiat that inspires you?" I ask.

"He was bold, unflinching. There is something beautiful in the way he peeled back his imagination to welcome us in. I think that exposing yourself like that is the equivalent of a writer finding her own voice."

I nod.

I ask her a few more questions to wrap up the interview, and her responses are straightforward. She has given me more than enough to write my article.

I take in the studio one last time, and I realize that I do not want to leave. I want to stand in this room, surrounded by her art. I want her to paint my body with her fingertips, recreating me with acrylic oils and perspiration.

She moves toward the door, edging me along, and when we reach the threshold of the basement stairs, I ask, "Can I ask you something off the record?"

She stops and faces me. "Sure."

"Do you think maybe I could take you out to dinner some time?"

She smiles uncomfortably, and I wish in that moment I could take back those words.

"I don't think that's such a good idea."

"I understand. You have a man."

"No, that's not it."

"I'm sorry. You have a woman."

She chuckles. "Nope. Not that either."

"Well, can I ask you what it is?"

"Ali, I just think it's inappropriate for you to ask me out after interviewing me."

I feel as though I have been kicked in my stomach with a steel-toed boot.

"And to be honest, I'm not attracted to you," she adds.

Her words stun me so quickly that I miss the first step going up and almost fall on the floor. "Shit!" I say, recovering my footing. "Well, okay. Thanks for the interview."

"No problem," she says.

She walks me up the stairs and escorts me to the front door.

I exit briskly without looking back.

I am deflated on the train ride back to my apartment, wanting to kick myself for how dumb I was about all of this. I still can't figure out how I allowed myself to become so infatuated with this woman in such a short period of time. And to make matters worse, I did this all at the expense of my relationship with my girlfriend.

I pick up my cell phone and call her, having no reason to doubt that she'll answer since she has the day off. She fails to pick up after several attempts, and I begin to wonder if we are really finished after all. It's difficult to know when you've had the last argument in a relationship like ours.

Maybe I need to just be alone and get my shit together. The past few days have taught me that I am apparently not satisfied with my current relationship, and the only fair thing for both of us would be to step back and give each other some space. Even as I toy with this thought, I can feel the loneliness setting in. In the past I was able to assuage this feeling by projecting my affections onto someone new. I had hoped that would be Riley Scott. Clearly, it is not.

What makes the situation sting even more is the brutal honesty with which she did it. That fearlessness she uses with her painting permeates throughout the other parts of her life, I see.

Yes, I definitely need time to be alone so I can figure out just where I want to be with things. My girlfriend would understand as much, given how things have been over this past year. Eventually we will talk, and this topic will come up, and we will discuss it and we will decide to go our separate ways for now. If things change in the future, so be it. But right now, neither of us is a good fit for the other.

By the time I reach my apartment, I am already exhausted from the morning's activities and want only to lie down. I walk into my bedroom and see the tube containing Riley's print resting on the chair next to my bed. I pick it up and place it in the back of my closet behind my dress shirts, in a dark corner, a place I could hopefully forget one day.

When I reach my bed, I take my phone out of my pocket and sit it on the desk. It starts to buzz immediately.

I glance at the display and see that it's my girlfriend.

I want to tell her that she is a wonderful person, but a relationship is probably not the right move for us. I pick up the phone.

"Hey, Ali. About this morning," she starts.

I want to tell her that it doesn't matter, but then I see the ruffled sheets on my bed and a faint strand of her hair on the pillow next to mine. I remember the warmth of her body, and things start to feel a little less empty.

"What are we doing?" she asks. "What kind of relationship do we have?"

This is the introduction I have wanted. This is where we part amicably and move on with our lives, but as I stand in my empty apartment, the coolness of the air settling over me, seeking to extinguish my tiny flame of hope, I cave.

"Come over," I say. "Let's talk about it."

I hear a rush of relief in her voice, and she consents.

"Ali?"

"Yeah."

"I love you."

I close my eyes, holding the phone to my mouth, my eyes set on the sheets before me, my body feeling warped like an overheated vinyl record. I can neither sense my mouth nor recognize my voice, but I hear the words clearly.

"I love you, too, baby."

Jessica and the Mattress

Jessica agreed to move in with me on one condition: I had to replace my mattress. We had been dating for two years, and this was the first time she had even mentioned that my mattress bothered her. If she had asked me to replace the bed frame or purchase a new headboard, I wouldn't have hesitated—I might've even understood—but she was asking me to go to the heart of the bed, the part that had seen me through the last ten years of my life, the part that had finally conformed to my body in such a way that I was now enjoying the best sleep of my life. She was asking me to make a sacrifice of incalculable measure.

See, to me, sleeping is more than the necessary recuperation of the body; it's my hobby. Some people collect coins or baseball cards. Others take cooking classes or pick up scuba diving. Me? I sleep. And when I say "sleep," I mean I get down and dirty with it. I own a special pair of socks, a lucky pillow (three smushed pillows squeezed into the same pillow case), and a comforter that my grandmother gave me as a high school graduation gift. I often propel myself through a trying day of working the grill at The Pit over at State University by thinking of how good the sleep will be when I finally get home. In fact, I believe I work even harder so that I can sleep even deeper.

The mattress was the first thing I bought when I moved out of my freshman dorm in college. There was nothing particularly special about it, but years of lying on it every-which-a-way, whether I was sharing it with someone or just lounging alone, broke it in the way an old car might be broken in by its owner. My father's 1993 pick-up truck has nearly 450,000 miles on the original engine, but he is the only one who knows the combination of jury-rigging necessary to get the thing to move down the street without cutting off. Like my father's truck, I am the only one who knows and, more importantly, appreciates the subtleties of my mattress, those lulls in the cushion where the springs have given way and cause you to roll toward the center of the bed.

And now Jessica wants me to abandon this mattress. It's like asking a man to give up being a fan of his favorite sports team, or even give up his religion.

As I stood listening to her request, she said in no uncertain terms that I had a choice to make: her or my mattress. I wish I could say that I labored over the decision—or even slept on it one last time—but in reality my response was reflexive, almost involuntary. Sometimes I still think about Jessica and miss her dearly, but knowing that I can put on my socks, grab my comforter, and jump into my bed for some of the best sleep of my life, makes the pain much more bearable.

The Illest

"Never love anyone who treats you like you're ordinary."

~ Oscar Wilde

Even after a week, Troy Dobbs still had yet to completely adjust to Aunt Flo's brownstone. It was far more spacious than the dorm room he had occupied over the past four years, and it was also much nicer than anything he had lived in, including his parents' house just off the bay in Gloucester, Virginia.

The decorations throughout the brownstone reflected an entirely different level of cultural sophistication than he was accustomed to. There were carved masks from Nairobi, signed prints by various African-American artists, and black & white photographs that were matted and framed featuring Aunt Flo alongside celebrities, politicians, and potentates. The furniture was sparse, yet fly, and ceiling-high bookcases stretched along two entire walls of the living room, packed with books from a myriad of African-American, Caribbean, and African writers. There was even a piece of a wood (part of a door maybe?) with Jean-Michel Basquiat's discernible handwriting, accompanied by his trademark crown. Against the rest of the artifacts of Aunt Flo's Cabinet of Curiosities, Troy didn't need to question its authenticity. He was, after all, in Brooklyn, and such things, as he was learning, were not completely unheard of.

The Notorious B.I.G. had passed away only three months earlier, and Brooklyn was wrestling with one of its most significant losses in years, yet it was still poised on the verge of declaring itself the new, undisputed capital of Planet Hip-Hop. Of course, Biggie's home neighborhood of Bed Stuy was a far cry from the Huxtable-like comfort of Aunt Flo's Brooklyn Heights neighborhood, but to Troy it was still *technically* Brooklyn and therefore good enough to embrace and throw his hands in the air whenever he heard Biggie rap the famous phrase, "Is Brooklyn in the house?"

Aunt Flo was out globetrotting with her latest male companion (a French model fifteen years her junior, Troy had heard), this time on a European cruise that departed from Barcelona. Her graduation gift to her only nephew was to leave the keys to her brownstone, a building of which she occupied all three floors (and basement) by herself, and have him housesit for the month that she would be away. And even though he had not yet gotten used to the amazing view of the skyline of Manhattan from the promenade view outside the kitchen window, he was gradually acclimating himself to the neighborhood, having found a breakfast diner on the corner of Henry and Clark and several great lunch and dinner spots along Montague Street.

His bedroom was on the second floor of the house, just off from the den area and down the hall from the kitchen. This was also the floor that housed the master bedroom and, from the clear look of things, the floor Aunt Flo occupied most. Artwork filled the halls, and personal photographs in small frames rested on the edges of freshly polished shelves.

Troy was not completely sure he knew what Aunt Flo did for a living, but he knew she had been married to a media mogul for ten years and had come away from that situation pretty well off. Since then she had become a bon vivant in a family full of people who neither had the time nor the interest in hedonistic socializing.

While Troy had been to Aunt Flo's home once several years back, he never imagined he would have the full run of the place. Each morning he awoke pinching himself and reminding himself of his amazing fortune. This awestruck state occupied most of his first week, and by the time he made it to Sunday morning, he had collapsed on the chaise lounge in the first floor library, a copy of Gloria Naylor's *Mama Day* opened across his chest, Coltrane's *A Love Supreme* playing softly in the background, telling himself he would one day have a place like this for his own.

The doorbell startled him, as the sound seemed to ring throughout every floor of the house all at once. He stirred, rolling himself off the chaise, and headed for the door. He wasn't expecting company—he didn't know anyone in New York—so he contemplated not answering the door. But wasn't the point of housesitting to let people know the house was being occupied? He reluctantly went to the door and pressed the intercom button.

"Yes?" he answered.

"Is Florence in?" a woman asked.

"She's out right now. I can take a message, though."

"I just came by to drop off a book I borrowed," the woman said.

"You can leave it with me, if you want."

"Who are *you*?"

"I'm Troy, her nephew. Can I ask who *you* are?"

"Eris."

Troy hesitated.

No way. It couldn't be. But he only knew of one person named Eris, and he thought he remembered seeing a picture of her in the house somewhere.

He nervously clicked the button to let her into the brownstone. Opening the second bolted door behind the front door, he watched in awe as Eris Perry walked into the room, a large coffee table book tucked under her arm. Troy wanted to smile nonchalantly, but his nerves got the better of him. He mentally settled on just trying to avoid coming off as wack.

"Hi, Eris," he said, unsure of what else to say.

She handed Troy the book, and he took it, examining the cover. It was a collection of nude photography by Marc Baptiste.

"So you like Marc Baptiste?" he asked.

"Yeah. He asked me to pose for his next book."

Troy couldn't believe what he was hearing. Eris Perry, with her beautiful, flawless deep brown complexion and the most incredible legs since Tina Turner, would be posing nude for Marc Baptiste. He did his best not to stare at her body through her orange and gold cotton sundress and the light scarf that hung from her neck, but because of the large tinted sunglasses she was wearing, he couldn't tell if she noticed him trying not to steal a glance at her.

"I think you'd be a great model," he said.

The exhalation from her mouth was part laugh, part sigh, as she shook her head. "So when will Flo be back?"

"She's in Barcelona about to take a 14-day cruise. She should be back at the end of the month. I'm housesitting for her."

He realized he was telling her a lot, but at this point he would have told her his social security number had she asked. This was Eris Perry, after all.

"Well, just tell her I came by," she said.

"Hold on," he said. "I didn't get a chance to offer you something to drink. I want to make sure I'm being hospitable."

"Nah, I'm good. Just tell Flo I came by."

"Yeah. Okay," he said. "I will."

Troy could feel the moment quickly slipping away as she headed toward the door.

"Hold on, Eris," he said. His nerves were finally settling out and now he was left only with the remnants of embarrassment.

She turned around, and he was unsure if she was perturbed by his attempts at delaying her departure. "Yeah?"

"I'm sorry. Can we start over? I'm Troy Dobbs, and I just graduated from Ellison-Wright College in Atlanta, and this is my first time being here in New York on my own, and I don't know anyone here, and it's been real quiet this first week, and, well, you're the first person I have had a conversation with since I've been here. I'm not gonna lie to you and say that being around a movie star like you isn't intimidating on some level, but on the real, this is the best thing that has happened to me since I arrived, and I guess I'm just trying to make it last as long as I can."

Eris listened to his rambling introduction and nodded. "It's cool," she finally responded. "I guess I can get some tea, if you don't mind."

Troy sighed. "Thanks. I really appreciate it, Ms. Perry."

"Just call me Eris," she said. "Troy, right?"

"Yes," he said, smiling at the fact she remembered his name. "Right up this way," he said, ushering her up the stairs to the second floor kitchen.

Eris took a seat at the table just off from the kitchen, while Troy pulled down the box of Tazo tea Aunt Flo kept in a cabinet next to the stove.

"Ellison-Wright College, huh?" she said.

"Yep. I finished last month with a major in mass communications."

"What do you plan on doing with that?"

"I just got accepted to USC for film school, so I'll be headed out there in August."

She smiled. "A filmmaker? Okay."

The obvious thing for him to do would be to ask her to be in one of his student films, but he fought the urge to come at her like that. From what little he knew about the costs associated with using a member of the Screen Actors Guild, he was unsure if that was even a possibility anyway. "So what are you working on these days?"

"I start shooting a new film in another month. Vancouver again," she responded.

"Must be nice," Troy said, setting the water kettle on the stove. "I think I've seen just about every movie you've been in."

"Thank you. But can I be straight up with you, Troy?"

"Sure."

"I don't really like to talk about work and all that stuff when I'm kicking back and chilling. All of my friends are good about this. Your aunt is one of my closest friends. She's been around the industry for a while and she's been like a mother figure to me since I moved to Brooklyn. She's definitely one of the people who helps keep things normal in my life."

Troy took down two mugs from the curio cabinet against the wall of the kitchen. "I had no idea my aunt was even cool like that."

"She's definitely cool like that."

"Okay. So movies are out. What is there to do around here? I've been to a few places, but I'm still branching out slowly," he said.

"This is New York. Honestly, you can do whatever you'd like."

"Well, what do *you* like to do?"

"Seriously?" she asked, biting her lower lip. "Probably walk down the street to the promenade and look across the East River. It's the best view of New York, bar none."

"So do you live in Brooklyn Heights?" Troy asked, pouring the water and then dropping in the tea bags. "Chai okay?"

"Sure. And no. I live in Fort Greene, but I like to come over here every other weekend for a change of scenery."

He placed the mugs on the table and sat down across from her. For a moment they sipped their teas in silence.

"I really appreciate your company," he said.

"No problem. I'm actually enjoying just chilling out."

"Well, if you ever want to come back by and hang out, I'm definitely available."

She laughed. "I'll keep that in mind."

When Eris finished her mug, she stood. "Well, it's been nice. I have to run."

Troy stood. "Yeah. I understand. It's been cool."

Eris nodded.

"Let me walk you out."

"Thanks," she responded, following him down the stairs.

Four hours later and Troy was still floored by the fact that he'd hosted Eris Perry in his aunt's brownstone. He had wanted to ask for her phone number, but didn't want to pressure her after things had gone so well. Plus, she knew how to reach him if she wanted to.

Troy had graduated from Coltrane to A Tribe Called Quest's *Beats, Rhymes and Life* album, with "1nce Again" looping on repeat. He tried to read more of his book, but he found his mind unable to sit still. Instead, he turned off the lights, reclined on the chaise lounge, and nodded off to the dopeness of the J. Dilla beat filling the room.

The Twin Towers punctuated the Monday evening skyline, the financial district glowing like a cluster of stars against the purple and pinkish hues of the evening sky. Across to the left, the Statue of Liberty stood in the sparkling blackness of the East River, almost like a rocket preparing to shoot off of Ellis Island and up into the dusky stratosphere. Troy stared in awe, his right hand planted firmly in his pocket, his fingers dancing along the nine and seven of the keychain he purchased several months ago alongside his graduation robe.

The gourmet ice cream in his cup was beginning to melt, and he wondered whether his introverted nature would cause him to miss out on what could be a great vacation. He had gone to the tourist-centric places, but hung back in the shadows, hoping to blend in with the locals. There were just *so* many people, none of them friends, associates, or even people with whom he would consider exploring his surroundings. It was then that this one reality dawned on him as he stared out into the night sky: for there to be eight million people who populated the metropolitan area of New York City, he could not possibly feel any lonelier than he did at that moment.

He knew Eris probably would not come by the brownstone until after Aunt Flo returned, and he doubted he would cross paths with her on the promenade either. Not now anyway. She had been the only person with whom he had shared any meaningful moment, and he dreaded that he might have come off as a starfucker in how he gushed over her.

When he returned to the brownstone, he picked up the phone and called his parents.

His mother answered in her warm, inviting voice on the second ring.

"Hello?"

"Mom," Troy said, hoping that his voice did not sound too winy.

"How are you doing, baby? How is Brooklyn treating you?"

"It's nice. How are you and Dad?"

"Oh, we're just fine. Your father's in the den watching some action movie on HBO. You know how he gets when he's watching his movies."

"Yeah," Troy said.

If he had been home with his parents, he would have been watching that movie with his father. It was part of their ritual and one of the reasons he fell in love with movies in the first place. When Troy's father found out that he had been accepted to film school, the old man could not have been any prouder.

"Are you okay?" his mother asked. "You sound a little down."

He started to lie to her, but his loneliness wouldn't allow him to. "It's just slow. I don't really know anyone here, and there's only so much I can do by myself. It's like going to Busch Gardens alone on the Fourth of July. You know what I mean?"

"I see," she responded. "I'm sure you'll find someone to do things with. You've only been there for a week."

"Well, I did meet someone yesterday, but I doubt I'll hear from her again before I leave."

"Why do you say that?"

"Because she's famous, Mom."

"Is that one of Flo's friends?"

"Yes."

They sat quietly on the phone for a few seconds.

"So are you going to tell me or do I have to ask?" his mother said.

Troy chuckled, enjoying the fact that his mother was not one for suspense, very much unlike his father. "It was Eris Perry."

"Are you talking about Victoria from that movie with Denzel?"

"That's her."

Troy found it curiously ironic that his mother only referred to actors by the names of characters they had played in movies she liked—well, actors other than Denzel—when she actually knew the actors' real names.

"Well, did you ask her out?"

Troy laughed. "Are you serious, Mom? This is Eris Perry we're talking about. What would I look like asking her out on a date?"

"Like a man who's interested in getting to know her better."

Troy started to respond, but he realized that his mother actually had a point. He could have asked her out, and while she might have turned him down, at least he would have known whether the mental energy he spent analyzing the previous day was really worth the effort.

The bottom line was that he was scared to ask her out. He knew that—and his mother probably knew that, although she would never say it directly to his face.

"I tell you what. If I see her again, I'll be sure to ask her out," Troy said.

"You do that," his mother responded. "And you know, if you wanted to, you could always lock up the brownstone and come back home for the rest of the summer. We'd love to have you here."

"Thanks, Mom, but I want to make the most of this opportunity. I'll still have a few weeks when I get home before I head out to Los Angeles, though. Maybe when I get back, Dad can gas up the boat and we can all go out on the bay and do some crabbing."

"That sounds like a plan."

"Okay. And Mom? Don't worry about me. I'll be just fine. Things have just been a little slow. That's all. I promise I'll get out and have an adventure tomorrow."

His mother's warm chuckle filled the phone, and he smiled.

"Well, I'm going to go and check on your father. I'll have him call you later this week."

"Sounds good."

Once Troy and his mother said goodbye, he took out the latest copies of *Time Out New York* and *The Village Voice*, the two periodicals Aunt Flo had told him to pick up when he arrived, and laid them down on the dining room table, side by side. He was determined to find activities to fill his week. There was no way he would allow himself to spend another week standing still.

By the time he lay down for bed, he made himself a promise that he would not allow his loneliness to affect the rest of his trip. He couldn't help being *alone*, but he realized that he did in fact have some control over whether or not he felt *lonely*.

Shortly after six o'clock the following evening Troy walked into the lobby of the Ambassador Theater. Monday had been black, the show's weekly night off, but Tuesday night was in full effect. People stood in line in front of the ticket and will-call windows. He had heard about rush tickets for *Bring in 'da Noise, Bring in 'da Funk* being available for $20, which was a bargain when it came to Broadway show prices. He purchased his ticket, and with a little over half an hour to blow in the meantime, he stepped outside of the theater and walked down toward the corner of 49th Street and Broadway. The city shone brightly with lights and activity for blocks, skyscrapers towering overhead from every angle, billboards touting various fashion brands and Broadway shows.

Finding a nearby building, Troy leaned his back against its warm brick facade, crossed his arms, and watched the activity around him. He was just as much a tourist as the people who poured over the sidewalks like ants emerging from a stomped anthill, but the filmmaker part of his personality preferred to maintain a kind of detached distance, taking in the view as if it were on a theater screen.

A mother held the hand of her toddler son, pulling him along the sidewalk, his little white sneakers determined to keep up. Passing them from the other side of the sidewalk was an older man, his smooth mahogany skin belying his white beard, his Gatsby hat slanted over his Afroed crown. Behind the older man was an Emo girl with blue hair and three piercings spaced across her bottom lip. Each of the people who passed Troy had a distinct style, and he wished he had his camera with him at that moment to capture what he was seeing. Instead, the camera sat in his bag back in Brooklyn, useless to him.

"I thought I was the only one who liked to people watch," a voice said, easing up beside him.

Troy turned his head, struggling to determine who this woman dressed in a lightweight military style jacket and a relaxed baseball cap pulled down low on her head was.

"Oh wow!" he said, reaching out to hug Eris.

She hugged him back.

"What are *you* doing out here?" Troy asked. "I almost didn't recognize you."

"This is my incog-*negro* outfit," she said, laughing. "I'm just waiting for my show to start. I have a friend in a play over at the Longacre Theatre. Are you catching a play anywhere around here tonight?"

"I'm going to see *Bring in 'da Noise*. Have you seen it?"

"Three times," Eris said, smiling. "It's really good! I don't think Savion Glover is doing the show right now, though. It seems like I remember reading somewhere that Bakari Wilder is doing his part. Either way, it'll be a good show if you've never seen it."

Troy nodded, unable to conceal the giant smile on his face. "I didn't think I was ever going to see you again before I left."

"Well, New York is a smaller place than you'd think. I'm sure you would have seen me at some point."

"I don't know," he responded, "but I was kinda hoping that I would."

"Why's that?"

"I enjoyed your company on Sunday, and, well, I was hoping that maybe we could hang out some time." He exhaled deeply, proud of himself for getting out the words. At least he fulfilled his promise to his mother to ask out Eris if he saw her again.

She nibbled on her bottom lip as she considered his words. "What are you doing after your show?" she finally asked.

"Nothing. Just wandering around Time Square before heading back to Brooklyn, I guess."

Eris glanced at her watch. "Meet me on the bottom level of the Virgin Megastore down the street at ten. Okay?"

"Sure," Troy said, nodding so enthusiastically he feared he might give himself whiplash.

"I'll be in the bookstore section near the magazine rack."

"Okay. I'll definitely be there."

"All right. Well, I have to head over to the theater. It's on the next street over. I'll catch up with you a little later."

"Most definitely," Troy responded, still unable to believe that she had not shut him down completely.

When he returned to the Ambassador and took his seat in the balcony, he was still smiling hard when the lights dimmed and the spotlight struck the first tap dancer.

Troy emerged from the theater still buzzing from the show. He had no idea of what the show was about and was surprised to learn that it was a retelling of the history of African Americans in the United States done purely through tap dancing, singing, and poetry. He was so in awe at times by what he had seen that he vowed to return and see the show again before he left New York.

The warm night air greeted him when he stepped back onto the street, and the realization that he would soon see Eris caused his heartbeat to quicken.

Just yesterday he was feeling crushed beneath his loneliness, and now his body was wrapped in euphoric bliss.

He walked to the corner of 49th Street and began his trek down to the Virgin Megastore off of Broadway and 46th Street. Part of him wanted to run the three blocks, but he realized that he still had about twenty minutes and that was time and distance he could use to calm his nerves. What would she want to do? Did it even matter? He was just happy to be in her company again.

For the briefest of moments he considered trying to find the Longacre Theater and meeting her when she came out of her show, but he didn't want to seem too eager. Plus, there was no guarantee she would come out of the theater through the main entrance or if she would take one of the side entrances used by the actors.

Instead, Troy walked the short distance to the Virgin Megastore, dodging the tourists who lined the streets, many of them standing completely still in the middle of the sidewalk, cameras pointed upward at various billboards. He pushed through the revolving doors to find an atrium full of music and people standing all around. Listening stations lined the walls and people held CDs to their faces as they nodded to the music coming from the huge black headphones cupping their ears. Troy quickly found the escalator and descended to the second floor.

More music and swag.

He continued on the escalator down to the third level. Off to his right were DVDs. Behind him, a movie theater. Straight ahead was a cafe, and off to his left was the bookstore with a magazine rack along the side wall. He considered going into the cafe and ordering a soda or something to calm his nerves, but he decided against it. With is luck, he might inadvertently burp from remnants of the carbonated water bubbling through his system, and that would be too difficult to recover from.

He walked into the bookstore section and began perusing the aisles. Restless, he finally eased over to the magazine rack and picked up a copy of *Vibe*. Toni Braxton stood naked on the cover, a towel covering her lower region, her hand crossing her breasts. Troy glanced at the title of the magazine to make sure he hadn't picked up a copy of *Playboy* by accident. Man, Toni had gone sexy, he thought, as he fanned through the pages to see the other pictures of her.

He didn't know how long he had been standing there, but when he glanced at his watch and saw it was nearly 10:40, he began to get the sinking feeling that Eris might have stood him up. He figured she must have had a Sidekick or cell phone or something, but without the number, he could do nothing more than wait. Placing the magazine back on the rack, he told himself that he would wait until 11 before heading down to the 42nd Street train station and catching the 2/3 line back to Brooklyn Heights.

Troy walked around the bookstore slowly, doubling back on the magazine rack several times. Still no Eris.

As he wandered around through the aisles, he thought back to the first movie he had ever seen of Eris Perry. She had played in a teenybopper update of a Shakespeare play where she was the best friend of the white brunette lead. Such roles seemed to be popular as Hollywood's version of diversity often depicted black people as sidekicks to white people, usually stealing scenes with their sass and humor. Eris was good at this when she got started, but then she did a movie where she was cast as a twenty-something lawyer named Victoria who fell in love with her married boss, played by Denzel Washington. That movie put her on the map, and since then, she had been working steadily.

With the DVDs directly across from the book section, Troy contemplated walking over there and checking to see which of Eris's movies might be in stock, but he stopped himself. He didn't want to get caught up in the fact that she was famous, although it was difficult not to.

As he waited, he began to get restless. Eris was the one who told him to meet her in this part of the store. She was also the one who had come by Aunt Flo's brownstone the other day and spent nearly half an hour chatting with him. Surely, she wasn't going to stand him up. Was she?

When Troy's watch showed 11 p.m., he reluctantly made his way to the escalator and began to ascend to the second level and then the first level. As soon as he stepped off, he saw her entering the store through the revolving door.

"Troy, I'm so sorry!" she said, walking up to him and hugging him. "I got held up with my friend. How long have you been here?"

"Since 10," he said.

"You've been waiting here the entire time?"

"Yeah, but it's no big deal. I was checking out some books and some music," he said. Truthfully, he was just happy that she'd shown up.

"I'm sorry," she repeated. "Have you eaten?"

"Not yet."

"Well, let's go get something to eat. My treat," she said. "It's the least I can do since you've been waiting here for a while."

"Sounds good to me," Troy responded.

As they walked outside and hopped in a cab, Troy had already forgiven her for showing up an hour late. The reality of the situation was that he was going out to dinner with Eris Perry at 11 p.m. on a Tuesday night in New York City. He couldn't have written a better script even if he tried.

Troy had never been to Murray Hill before, and the quaint Manhattan-esque resident brownstones blending with mom-and-pop businesses scattered throughout the neighborhood surprised him even more by having a restaurant that was still open. The cab had zoomed east and delivered them to the door of a small Italian restaurant nestled between two other businesses and tucked down a set of stone stairs. The entire ride over had taken less than ten minutes.

"Come on," she said, walking down the stairs and opening the door.

Troy, still in awe, rushed to keep up with her.

"This way," a young guy dressed in black said, escorting the two of them to a table in the back corner of the restaurant.

The rugged red brick pattern across the wall gave the place the aura of a wealthy person's wine cellar.

Candlelight flickered from the tabletops scattered across the small room, but the overhead light still provided a modest glow.

Eris navigated easily through the maze of tables and chairs, leaving Troy to believe this was one of her usual spots.

"Nice and cozy," Troy offered, after they took their seats.

"Yeah. I like it here."

He almost said, "Do you come here often," but he realized how horribly cliché that comment was and instead asked, "How was your friend's play?"

Eris smiled, and it felt to Troy like the room brightened a bit more. "It was nice. He did an amazing job! When I see plays like that, it makes me think about returning to the stage soon. I'd have to find the right play and set aside time to do it, though."

Troy didn't know why he had assumed Eris's friend was a woman, not that it should have mattered, he figured. Still, he could feel the dull ache of insecurity throbbing in his temples. He tried not to let his disappointment seep into the conversation. "I would love to see you in a play. I think you'd be great."

"Thank you, Troy."

The server returned to the table to take their orders, and Eris ordered a salad, while Troy ordered an appetizer of fried calamari.

When the server left, Eris continued. "So what did you think of *Bring in 'da Noise*?"

"Off the hook! I've never seen anything like it. To be honest, I thought about tap dancing like it was some white girl 'chorus line' kind of thing. But these guys were raw. Straight up beasts! They took the game to a whole new level."

Eris nodded. "I'm glad you liked it. Last year Savion Glover won a Tony for choreography. That cast is so talented! I'm amazed they can do that show night after night."

"Yeah," Troy said, "it seems like it would take a lot out of you, physically and emotionally. I see why people keep going back to see it over and over."

"Guilty as charged," Eris said, raising her hand.

Troy looked at her as she spoke, trying to remove the idea of her being a famous actress from his head. She was just a cool woman sitting across the table from him. She put on her pants one leg at a time, right? It was not beyond belief that they would have shared interests, was it? He took a deep breath and told himself that if he wanted to get to know her better, he could not allow her fame to distract him from doing so.

Then it happened.

She sneezed.

It was light but distinctive. In fact, it sounded like a small animal blowing a miniature party favor. It was cute-sounding and funny at the same time, and when Eris covered her mouth bashfully, excusing herself, Troy understood that she was just a regular person with regular person idiosyncrasies, and he could feel a burden lift from his shoulders.

They continued conversing until the food arrived and then continued afterwards. She told him about how she started acting and how she one day wanted to direct. She worried about the small number of black women who were directing and how the industry was biased against older women. She pondered what that would mean for her career down the road. The fear of her future pushed her to do more films now, but she had to be careful to do roles that would mean something years from now and roles that would not set back the achievements of other black actresses. "It's more of a burden than you'd think. You want to hear something funny? I always wonder what someone like Ruby Dee would think of my role in a particular movie. I don't know why I do that. Ruby Dee will probably never watch most of my films, but I think she's amazing and I don't want her to one day finally see one of my films and think that I set black women back fifty years. I know that probably doesn't make much sense, does it?"

Troy found her insecurities endearing and felt relieved that she could confide these things to him so easily. "It makes sense, but I doubt you'd have anything to worry about. I'm sure she'd be proud of you."

Eris smiled and placed her hand on top of his. "I appreciate you saying that."

The feel of her hand touching his made him want to dance around the table, but he played it cool, keeping his hand as still as he could for as long as she wanted her hand to be there.

"So what do you like to do when you're not working?" he asked.

"You know, I would've said travel. That's what I would have said if you had asked me before things really picked up with my work. When I was younger, all I wanted to do was travel the world. I actually wrote in my diary that I wanted to go to at least one hundred countries!"

"Have you been to a hundred countries?"

"More than a hundred. And sadly, I have only been to ten or so where I was actually able to kick back and really take in the culture without being connected to some project or the promotion for some project." She paused as she considered her own words. "I guess it's like a monkey's paw kind of irony: you want to see the world, but you wind up seeing most of it from a suitcase and a hotel window."

Troy started to say that he understood, but he had never travel as extensively as she had and felt that he was ill-equipped to co-sign on her statement. Instead, he said, "You said traveling is what you would have said if I asked you back in the day, but I'm asking you right now. What do you like to do with your free time now that you're, well, who you are?"

She smiled. "I've learned that simplicity best suits me when I have down time. A good book and a fluffy pillow are heaven. Just being still, you know?"

On this, he did understand. "Do you have a favorite author?"

"Gloria Naylor. I will read anything that she writes."

"You've got to be kidding me!" Troy said, breaking out into a broad smile. "I'm reading *Mama Day* right now."

"For real? That's my favorite book. I even gave a copy of it to Flo."

"That must be the one I'm reading then," he responded, suddenly feeling the emotional distance between he and Eris become exponentially shorter. It was like by reading her book, he was allowed a glimpse into an intimate space in her world.

"You'll have to let me know what you think of it. It's a beautiful story of love and sacrifice and one of the few books I've read that actually made me break out a box of Kleenex."

"It's like that?"

She nodded.

"So you and my aunt must be pretty close if you gave her a copy of your favorite book," he said between bites of his food.

"She's one of my best friends." Eris allowed the words to hang in the air, giving them full gravity, which only made Troy more curious.

"How did you meet Aunt Flo? I have to admit I'm pretty surprised that the two of you even know each other."

Eris burst into laughter, lowering her face and covering her mouth with her hand. She laughed hard, rocking back in her seat, the corners of her eyes moistening. Troy stared on in befuddlement, having no idea of what he had said that would elicit this kind of response. Was she laughing at him or something he said? His insecurities emerged and thickened the air around him.

"I'm sorry," she finally managed. "It's just that I'm not used to someone saying 'Aunt Flo' about an actual person."

Troy shrugged his shoulders. "I don't get it."

"Well, you're a guy, so maybe you wouldn't. To a woman, Aunt Flo is a monthly visitor."

He thought about it for a second. Then he blurted out, "Oh, a period?"

In the moment he heard his voice and saw the huge, embarrassed smile on Eris's face, he realized that he had missed the cue to use discretion on the topic. He mumbled the words "Aunt Flo" to himself quietly, deciding then that he needed to have another name for his mother's sister. He reasoned that he would call her Flo when talking to Eris, as it was awkward for him to say Aunt Florence, a name that only put him in the mindset of *The Jeffersons* TV show and the sassy maid of the same name. Plus, the name Florence felt too formal for such a laid back and cool woman.

Eris inhaled deeply, her laughter petering out into light exhalations. "I met Flo about six years ago. At the time, she was married to Dante Wilbourne over at Viacom. We were at a party down in SoHo and were introduced by a mutual friend. Truth be told, I just thought she would be someone I knew in passing, but that night we were both wearing handbags by the same designer, so we got into a conversation about that. By the end of the night, we had moved on to talking about books and what it was like for each of us moving to New York from The South. We just hit it off.

"After that, we would get together for lunch sometimes, and I guess we just got to a point where we trusted each other. When her marriage to Dante was on the rocks, I did my best to be there for her. Then later on when I was going through a situation with this guy I was dating, and things were pretty ugly, she was there for me, helping *me* through it. We've been through a lot together, and she's one of the few people on this planet that I actually trust. She's like an older sister to me, and frankly, at this point in my life, I don't know what I'd do without her."

"Is that why you took me up on the tea this past Sunday?" Troy asked.

"You kind of put everything out there when I was leaving, and I thought to myself that you seemed like a nice enough guy to talk to for a few minutes. But I'm not gonna lie. If you had been anyone else's nephew, I probably would have kept it moving right along."

He nodded, for once appreciating his proximity to Flo, while feeling slightly deflated that her kindness was more the result of nepotism than his own charm.

Once the bill came, Troy offered to pay.

"I told you earlier. I got this," Eris said, sliding her hand around his and gripping the leather-encased bill.

"Well, thank you," he responded. "At least let me pick up the tip then."

Eris chuckled, her voice almost musical. "I take it you're not used to women paying for the meal."

"Truthfully? No."

"Well, sit back and enjoy it. I'm sure you'll be back to paying for meals in no time."

He laughed to himself. "Probably."

They walked outside into the warm night air, and Troy glanced down at his watch. It was almost 1 a.m., but he was not ready for the evening to end just yet. He waited for a moment to see what Eris wanted to do, and when she didn't say anything, he asked, "Feel like going for a walk?"

"Sure."

As they walked past the brownstones lining either side of the street, Troy began to wonder if this was in fact a date. It felt intimate and comfortable in the way that a date in Atlanta would have felt. The last date he had been on was a week before graduation and it was with another graduating senior named Beulah (a name he couldn't seem to match to her face). It was more of a "farewell/sorry we never hooked up in college" kind of date that ended with awkward, regrettable sex. Needless to say, he was still enjoying his evening with Eris and things were going ten times better than they did at the height of his date with Beulah.

"I can't see how Bad Boy is gonna survive without Biggie. You can't possibly mean that Puffy is gonna sell any records off his new album," Troy said.

"Puff is an entertainer, if ever there were one. Watch and see. He's probably gonna sell more records than any other artist on Bad Boy," Eris responded.

"But he can't rap!"

"I have a feeling that won't matter too much if his tracks are hot."

"Eris, as much as I want you to be right, I think you're overestimating him. He's a business guy, not a rapper. That album is gonna tank like the Exxon Valdez."

She laughed. "We'll see."

"You know," Troy said, pacing his steps to correspond evenly with hers, "this has been really cool—spending time with you."

Eris nodded. "You're not so bad yourself."

"Do you think maybe we could do this again—soon?"

"Okay."

At that moment, he reached for her hand and stopped her in her tracks. Standing beneath the overarching canopy of a small tree, he said, "I have a question to ask you. Is this a date?"

Eris chuckled and looked away, shrugging her shoulders. "Aren't we just hanging out? Two people enjoying each other's company."

"It feels like more. I know this is going to sound crazy, but I feel like I should kiss you right now."

"Oh, you do? What's giving you that vibe?"

"I don't know. *This. Here. Right now.* If this isn't a date, this would definitely be the best non-date of my life."

"You like to overthink things, don't you," Eris said, continuing to walk down the sidewalk.

Troy quickly caught up to her, now feeling slightly embarrassed. Was he supposed to have not said anything and just kiss her? He didn't know, but he was determined to find out.

He reached for her hand again, and when she turned to face him, he leaned in and kissed her softly on her lips. She chuckled softly to herself, her eyes registering a mild surprise. For the life of him, he could not tell what she was thinking now that he had acted.

"That was nice," she finally said.

He leaned in to kiss her again, but she placed a hand on his chest, pushing him back. "Easy, Loverboy."

"Did I do something wrong?" he asked.

"No, but I think we need to call it an evening."

Troy waited for her to say she was just kidding. After all, they had only walked two blocks from the restaurant. Maybe he wasn't supposed to kiss her after all.

"Are you *sure* I didn't do something wrong?" he asked again.

"You're cool," she offered nonchalantly.

"Can I get your number and call you some time then?" he asked.

"Don't worry. I know how to contact you."

She stepped between two parked cars and lifted her hand, hailing a passing taxi. When the vehicle stopped, she looked back. "I enjoyed dinner."

"Yeah, it was nice."

Troy was stunned as Eris got into the cab and it rolled off into the night.

Standing there on the street with nothing but the muted sounds of the city around him, he wondered what had gone wrong. Why had she left him all alone on a dark street? She had picked him up, fed him, and dropped him off on the corner like a used-up, snot-filled rag, and while a part of him would have rejoiced in being a part of her world for the few hours of magic they shared, the other part of him felt betrayed, let down, and disappointed.

By the time he reached the train station and took a seat on the bench to wait indefinitely for the next train to come, he almost believed everything he had just experienced was a dream—a really bad dream—but he knew the truth: he was awake, in a tunnel below ground, and Eris, in all of her glorious splendor, was now gone.

Troy awoke, stretched out perpendicularly across his bed, the sun blazing through the room's blinds. He glanced at the digital clock on the nightstand, surprised to see that it was nearly 1 p.m. He could scarcely remember how he made it home. All he could make out was that he had waited nearly half an hour for the train and had fallen asleep on the ride home, nearly missing his stop. How he made it up the stairs to the his bedroom on the second floor of Flo's brownstone was beyond him.

As soon as he placed his feet on the floor and stood up, the thought of the dinner with Eris filled his head. It had all ended so weirdly. Even as he stumbled into the shower, he still had an "out of sync" feeling about all that had happened. He had totally misread her body language. Still, she had allowed him that first kiss. Maybe there was much more to it than she was willing to tell him.

Flo had a computer in one of the bedrooms that had been converted into an office space, so Troy logged on to the Internet and went to Yahoo! to search for anything he could find on Eris. Mainly, he wanted to know if she was romantically involved with anyone. He didn't know if they put those kinds of things on the Internet, but he imagined it would be pretty cool if they did. When his search came up empty, save the few things about her films, he resigned himself to the fact that he would just have to let the situation play out on its own. Maybe she would call; maybe she wouldn't. Either way, he would have to be okay with that.

Once he had brushed his teeth and gotten dressed, he walked downstairs to the library, picked up the copy of *Mama Day* he had been reading, the one Eris had given Flo, and stretched out on the chaise lounge.

He had to stop and reread every other paragraph because his mind kept drifting. Was Eris thinking about last night like he was? What did she want from him?

The dinner had been her idea. In fact, every major element of the time they had been around each other since they met she had overseen. Maybe he was just a temporary escape from the life she knew. Most of her friends and associates were probably connected to the entertainment industry. He was just a mass communications grad from a small black college in Atlanta, and for the moment, at least, he was unconnected to her world. He was just a guy on vacation taking in the beauty of New York.

Unable to still his mind, Troy stood up, tossing the book on the chaise. He returned to his bedroom and packed a notebook and camera into his backpack. He would just go exploring today, he figured. Grabbing his wallet and keys from the dresser beside the bed, he headed downstairs, locked up the brownstone, and started his trek across the Brooklyn Bridge into Manhattan.

"What exactly is *celebrity*?" Troy pondered, as he navigated the streets of the financial district. Was it the fact that your face and your art were ubiquitous to a particular population? Did it make those people really any different from people who did not have the same level of exposure? After all, celebrities were just doing their jobs, and it just so happened that those jobs were just more high profile than others. But if celebrities were just high profile workers, why did so many people clamor for fame or the chance to be scrutinized by the general populous? Maybe it had to do with money—or better yet the misperception that fame and wealth were conjoined. Just a glance at many of the rappers perpetuating the illusion of wealth because their record labels forced them to do a Hype Williams video was enough to make one wonder if there was some form of social security plan for the celebrity whose fame had expired before his bank account birthed a positive integer.

Troy cared increasingly less about Eris's *celebrity* and next to nothing about whether her talents had netted her a healthy income. All he knew was that he was becoming more enamored with her, the same as he would a sista he had been heavily scoping on the yard at Ellison-Wright. This was a difficult notion to juxtapose with her awkward departure from the previous evening, though.

If he were to focus on everything from the moment he saw her on the corner of 49th and Broadway until the moment they walked out of the Italian restaurant, he would have slept soundly, blissfully even, but those last minutes were impossible to ignore. For every minute he sat in the bowels of the Metro station waiting for a train to come in the wee hours of the morning, he felt the compounding sting of her abrupt departure. Maybe the kiss was too much.

The kiss was probably too much.

But hadn't she kissed him back? And hadn't she said that it was nice? Wouldn't that have been an invitation to continue?

As Troy removed the SLR camera from his backpack and attached the zoom lens, it began to dawn on him that maybe he had not done anything wrong after all. Maybe Eris's conflicts were of a more ambivalent and personal nature and had little to do with him. Troy considered this for a moment, but it did not provide him the kind of relief he so desperately craved.

Pointing his camera at the Brooklyn Heights promenade, he began snapping shot after shot. From the other side of the East River, it was easy to think the entire view of things was Manhattan-centric. Seeing his neighborhood from Manhattan, however, provided him a fresher perspective. The view was different, low-key. Beautiful.

He could hardly make out the people on the promenade and wondered briefly if perhaps Eris was walking along the brick path looking casually across the East River to where he stood. He would need binoculars, definitely something much stronger than his lens, to know if that were true, but he doubted it. After last night he was unsure of whether their paths would ever cross during his remaining weeks in Brooklyn.

It had been magical, yes. Brief and inviting? Yes. But was it destined to be more than an incredibly surreal, yet singular, occurrence? Probably not.

Once Troy finished taking pictures, he caught a train up to the Village, had a slice of pizza, and returned back to Flo's place, content to spend the rest of the afternoon reading and listening to music. He was, after all, on vacation, and he knew that USC would provide him with little time to rest in the fall.

As Troy climbed the steps of the brownstone, he noticed a folded sheet of paper taped to the front door. He quickly peeled it away and opened it.

Troy,
I was in the neighborhood and just dropped by to see if you were around. Call me when you get a minute. (718) 555-2235.
Eris.

She had come back after all. And she had left him a phone number.

Troy had been mentally preparing himself to accept the fact that he would never see her again, except maybe on the big screen, but the note, in its beautiful cursive penmanship, begged to differ.

He examined the sheet of paper looking for a time. She might still be in the neighborhood, he thought, as he trotted down the stairs and over to the promenade. Had she really been there while his lens was pointed in this direction?

He scanned the length of the promenade looking for Eris and then for people who might have been Eris in disguise. The only people he saw, however, were the usual people from the neighborhood, the regulars who walked their dogs, jogged, or lazed about the benches daily.

He walked back around to Henry Street and headed for Montague, but once he reached the ice cream parlor there, he knew that he would never be able to find her among the hundreds of people scattered sporadically down the street going toward Fulton Street. He had simply missed her.

Still, there was the phone number, something that assured him that they would be able to reconnect regardless.

He trotted back to the brownstone, raced upstairs, and picked up the phone.

The phone rang several times before Eris answered.

"Troy?" she said.

He blushed at the thought that she had been anticipating his call to the point she would answer with his name.

"How did you know?" he said, more as a play of modesty than anything else.

"Flo's number is in my phone already. It came up on the screen."

Troy chuckled to cover his embarrassment, reminding himself that he was *still* on the phone talking to Eris—which had to be pretty damn spectacular, given the situation.

"I just got back to the house. When did you come through?" he asked.

"Oh, I passed through around noon. I was just in the neighborhood and decided to drop in and check on you."

She said it like she was doing Flo a favor and had no personal interest invested in the situation. Troy found this a bit difficult to believe, though.

"I hate that I missed you. It would have been nice seeing you again."

"Yeah," she said.

He could not tell if she was being nice or genuine.

"I'm free for the rest of the evening—if you wanted to hook up and hang out," he offered.

"Hold on," she said, stepping away from the phone.

He waited for nearly two minutes before she returned.

"Wanna go to this event with me tonight?" she asked. "It's a fashion show for Fila or something like that."

Troy grinned so widely that he felt his face aching from the stretch. "Sure. Just tell me when to be ready."

"The invite says seven, but I know the show won't start until closer to eight. I can have the car come by and get you around 6:30."

"But how should I dress?"

"It's a fashion show. Just wear something chill. There'll probably be a DJ, an open bar, and a lot industry people there. I'm wearing a designer tee, jeans, stilettos, and one of my bags."

"Oh," Troy said, suddenly realizing that this was the kind of event that was actually several levels above his present social station. There would be celebrities there, he knew, and with him arriving with Eris, he would need to really dig into his vault of confidence to pull this off. For a split second, he almost asked if he could bail out, but he knew she would never present him with the opportunity unless she really wanted him to go. He would just have to suck it up and pull himself together. "I'll be ready," he finally said.

"Okay. I'll see you then."

He hung up the phone and looked at the clock. It was nearly 4:00 p.m., definitely not a lot of time to calm his nerves.

He hopped in the shower and started brainstorming what he had in his suitcase that he could wear, since he didn't have enough time to go out and buy anything. By the time he dried off, he had pieced together his wardrobe in his head. He would wear a white dress shirt, a pair of dark, dressy denims, his black leather loafers and matching belt, and a navy blue blazer. While he didn't consider himself a fashion aficionado, he had learned at Ellison-Wright that there were core staples a man should always travel with, especially if he were gone for longer than a day. Of course, he had not intended to wear *that* particular combination at any point; still, he was pleasantly surprised such seemingly arbitrary advice could prove so instrumental in a bind like this.

He finished dressing around 5:30 and headed into the kitchen to grab a snack, just in case it was a while before he ate again. Then he went downstairs to wait in the library.

Looking around the quiet room, Troy could feel his pulse quickening. What if he said the wrong thing or did the wrong thing? It was one thing to do something foolish in the presence of Eris, but it was another thing to do something publicly that could embarrass both of them. The fact that they would be going together meant that, at least publicly, they were somewhat of a couple— if only for the evening. Last week if someone told him he would be escorting the most beautiful actress in Hollywood to a fashion show, he would have slapped the person who was doing the talking. No one dared dream that big!

Troy could see the Lincoln Town Car through the front window when it pulled up. He locked up the brownstone and walked down the steps. The car's windows were tinted, and by the time he pulled the handle of its door, his stomach was in knots. He looked into the car and immediately realized it was empty.

"Excuse me," Troy said in the direction of the driver. "Who sent this car?"

"Sir, my dispatcher sent me to this address. I'm supposed to pick you up and take you to 41st and 6th in the city. That's all I know."

Troy stared at the empty backseat, wondering where Eris was. Hadn't she said that she was coming to pick him up? Or had she said that she was sending a car to get him? He couldn't remember.

"Sir, are you getting in?" the driver asked. He was attempting to be polite, but it was clear that he was becoming annoyed with this kid who didn't seem to appreciate having a driver take him into the city.

"Yes," Troy responded, hopping into the backseat. So this was how it was going to play out, he thought, as the driver navigated the neighborhood then onto the Brooklyn Bridge.

Seeing New York City from a car was refreshing. The evening sun gave a golden tint to the buildings, and as the car sped along the streets, Troy noticed pedestrians moving about the sidewalks and sighed that he was not one of them. The plush comfort of the town car added to the fact that this was not just a taxi ride where plopping your behind in the seat cost $2.00—that is, if you were able to catch a cab as a black man.

The Town Car pulled up to a stop outside of a nondescript brick building, where a short line of people stood in line behind a red velvet rope. They were flashing passes and the bouncer was admitting them one by one. It was then that Troy realized he didn't have a pass.

"Excuse me," he said to the driver. "Did the person who sent this car for me leave a package with you to give me?"

"No, sir. No package. I was just told to drop you off here."

Troy stepped out of the car and walked toward the line. It was moving quickly, and he realized he would be face-to-face with the bouncer, empty-handed, in a matter of seconds. He quickly stepped out of line and walked to the pay phone on the corner, retrieved Eris's phone number, and called her.

His call went straight to voicemail. "Hey, Eris, I just wanted to let you know that I was here. I'm standing outside the club waiting for you. I don't have a cell phone, so I'll just be out front waiting." He hung up and walked back to the club.

A limousine pulled up in front of the building, and Z, a famous supermodel, stepped out and was quickly ushered through the door. Troy went back to the line behind the rope, trying to play it cool, although the June air was starting to make him sweat.

"Pass?" the bouncer said, holding out his hand to Troy once he'd reached the front of the line.

"I'm a guest of Eris Perry's," he said. "I might be on a list or something."

The bouncer, a huge Puerto Rican guy with muscles jumping through his black designer t-shirt, lowered his head, scanning the list. "What's your name?"

"Troy Dobbs."

The bouncer looked up and down the different pages of his clipboard before saying, "No Troy Dobbs on the list."

"What should I do? Eris Perry had a car drop me off here to meet her."

"Yeah, and Janet Jackson is giving me a ride home tonight," the bouncer said, laughing. "Step to the side, kid."

Troy stepped out of line, his face flush with embarrassment, his body sticky with sweat. He glanced at his watch. It was 7:15, and he figured surely Eris should know by now that he'd arrived. Frustrated, he walked across the street and leaned against the building facing the club.

Over the next ten minutes, Town Car after Town Car, limousine after limousine, pulled up dropping off a Who's Who list of celebrities at the front door. At a certain point Troy lost track of who was in the building, but he figured the list of famous people rivaled that of a major awards show. All he knew was that he was still outside, his blazer now resting in the crook of his arm, his dress shirt sleeves cuffed to his elbows. His feet were starting to hurt from standing so long in his loafers, and he contemplated just how much longer he would wait outside the club before walking down to the Metro Station a few blocks away and heading back to Brooklyn.

He glanced at his watch again. He would leave at 7:30, he told himself.

Once the long hand of his watch touched the numeral six, he took one last look at the door. Surely she would come to get him. It would have been pointless to have a car bring him this far just to drop him off and leave him. He turned to leave.

That's when he saw a thin woman with an Afro emerge from the club, wielding a Sidekick and looking frantically from left to right. It took a moment before she looked straight ahead in Troy's direction. He stood still, unsure of whether she was walking towards him or simply crossing the street.

"Troy?" she said.

"Yes."

"I'm Regina, Eris's assistant. We've been looking all over the place for you. Have you been out here the entire time?"

Troy reached up dramatically and wiped the sweat from his brow. "Yeah. I've been out here for a while. I was actually just about to leave."

"Don't do that. Come with me. The show hasn't started yet. Eris has been waiting on you since seven."

Troy sighed and considered telling Regina that he'd pass. He was tired and felt sticky. His coolness had expired the moment he had to take off his jacket and cuff his sleeves.

"I'm really sorry," Regina added. "Things got mixed up. I only knew to come out here because we called the car service, and they said that you had already been dropped off."

Troy looked around him, noting that all of the activity was straight ahead. The party was directly in front of him, and he already knew the myriad of entertainers in the building because he had seen them all arrive. It was definitely tempting. But he realized all of that paled in comparison to the fact that Eris had been waiting on him, refusing to stop looking for him when he didn't arrive. Although the situation had been horribly inconvenient, one thing seemed clear, as far as Troy was concerned: Eris actually cared about him.

He looked into Regina's expectant eyes and nodded. "Okay. Let's go."

Regina smiled and walked back to the bouncer.

"He's with Eris Perry," she said to the bouncer, pointing at Troy, whose clothes were damp with sweat.

Troy did his best to be cool and nod his head like, "I told you so."

The bouncer looked at Troy and said, "Oh word? My bad, my man." He then stepped aside and let Regina and Troy into the building.

Behind Troy he could see that the sun was starting to set.

Regina handed him a paper napkin from her purse without saying a word. This only amplified how humiliated Troy was that he had to stand outside long enough to sweat through most of what he was wearing. The air conditioning inside the club was a welcome reprieve, and once he wiped his brow with the napkin, he realized that he would probably be dry by the time the show ended.

Regina led him through the throng of A, B, and C-listers. Supermodel Z was chatting with Puffy, while Isaac Hayes escorted his date to a seat near the stage. When Troy got within range of Eris, his heart melted like a popsicle lying on a Mississippi sidewalk in July. This was the first time he had seen her really looking like the *movie star* Eris Perry.

Eris was famous for a particular bob hairstyle, where her hair was faded in the back. The cut was so connected to her image, it was often referred to as the Eris Perry cut, in the way the Halle Berry's hairstyle was referred to as the Halle Berry cut. With the makeup and that glow of celebrity, Eris looked different than she had when Troy had hung out with her days before. She had been low key with the hats and loose clothing, but now this was Eris Perry in all of her famed glory. The sight of her put Troy in so much awe that if he died at that moment, he would have sailed into the great beyond a very satisfied man.

When Eris noticed Troy approaching, her lips gave way to a smile. She was smiling for *him*, Troy thought, unable to hide his own smile. She stood and embraced him.

"I'm so glad Regina was able to find you. I was starting to get worried that the car service had broken down or something."

He started to recap the last forty-five minutes of standing outside getting dissed by the bouncer in the hot June sun, but then he decided to let it go. After all, she had just embraced his damp body and not commented on it. She knew, just like he knew, that everything that had happened was unfortunate, and her willingness to move forward with the evening inspired him to do the same.

"It was an adventure—but I made it. Just in time." He smiled so she would know there were no hard feelings.

"I see you met my assistant, Regina."

"Yeah. She's cool people."

Regina took a seat on the other side of Eris, leaving Eris and Troy to converse privately.

"I'm just glad to be here with you," Troy said, taking in all of her beauty up close.

She reached out and squeezed his hand. "I just hope you enjoy the show."

"I'm sure I will."

The lights dimmed and the runway lit up with model after model walking the runway wearing the latest in the fall sport collection of Fila, a brand that Troy had once enjoyed as a child, particularly when it was an Italian import. From what he was hearing, though, there were some trademark issues and now there was a rebranding of the U.S. version. He half-expected Z to model in the show, but she was clearly a supermodel and in attendance primarily as a celebrity, which was further enhanced by the fact that she sat next to Puffy.

Troy found it difficult to really pay attention to the models on the runway. All he thought about was what would it be like to have a space like this to himself with Eris. She was the model walking through the runway of his mind, and truth be told, it did not matter what label she was wearing or from what collection.

The fashion show didn't last long, and within minutes the DJ had started spinning tunes for those who wished to remain afterwards. Many of the celebrities were already at the coat check, preparing to leave for other events. Eris leaned over and whispered something to Regina, who nodded and walked away. Eris then approached Troy.

"So what did you think of the show?" she asked.

"Pretty cool. Thanks for bringing me."

"No problem. I'm just sorry you had to wait outside so long." She patted his chest. "But at least now you're dry," she said, chuckling.

He allowed himself to smile, silently appreciating the fact that his shirt was no longer sticking to him.

The DJ started playing "Runnin'" by Pharcyde, and Troy found himself involuntarily nodding to the rhythm of the music.

"You wanna dance?" Eris asked.

"Are you serious?"

"Or are Ellison-Wright men too good to dance?"

Troy laughed, taking her hand and guiding her onto the dance floor, where several other celebrities and socialites had already gathered to dance. He loved the song and found himself rapping along with it. Eris smiled, watching him as he moved from side to side, matching him with her own smooth movements.

The DJ mixed in several other songs, and they continued dancing, but when Troy felt the first beads of sweat forming on his forehead, he slowed down to a basic two-step. There was no way he would allow himself to sweat through his clothes a second time.

"What do you have planned for the rest of the evening?" Troy asked.

"I don't know. What's up?"

"I was just hoping the evening wouldn't have end here."

Eris smiled. "You don't hold back, do you?"

"What do you mean?"

"You're pretty straight forward with what you want."

Troy shrugged his shoulders. "I don't know. I guess it always feels like it might be the last time I see you whenever we're together, so I want to at least put it out there for you so you'd never be able to say you didn't know what I was thinking."

"I can appreciate that. Let's go."

Troy didn't even bother to ask where. He would have gone anywhere she asked him to go.

The Town Car dropped them off on 6th Avenue, near 30 Rockefeller Plaza. Troy thought it an odd choice, given the general popularity of the location, but he was happy to be in such a beautiful architectural space with Eris.

They walked between skyscrapers toward the overlook, where flags surrounded a courtyard that would serve as an ice skating rink in the winter. They took a seat on one of the benches between the two buildings situated just behind the overlook.

"When I first moved to New York, I came here," Eris said. "There were hundreds of people walking around here and down there in the courtyard." She pointed just beyond them at the pit that lay ahead, all of the tourist activity taking place on a lower structural level. "You know, people told me that I would never make it in the industry living in New York. 'You have to move to L.A.,' they kept saying. But I've always been in love with this city—ever since I was a little girl and used to see it on TV."

Troy nodded. "You're from Louisiana, right?"

Ellis smiled, nodding. "Small place called Monroe, somewhere along I-20 between Mississippi and Texas."

"When did you come here?"

"As soon as I graduated from high school. There was only so much I could do at home. Booking local commercials and doing community theater got kind of old after a while. My mom thought I was crazy for coming here. She wanted me to go to Xavier University in New Orleans and major in biology or something. I swear I thought she would disown me when I turned down the scholarship offers for school. In the end, it was my dad who convinced her that I could just defer for a year and see what happened with my acting. I think they both figured the 'real world' would shock me back into school faster than Flo Jo doing 100 meters, but they were wrong. I had no intention of ever going back—not if I could help it."

"So how long have you been in New York?" Troy asked.

"Long enough."

"Seriously. How long?"

"Going on fifteen years," she said, chuckling. "I guess that's long enough for me to know that I probably won't be going to college."

Troy quickly surmised that Eris was around thirty-three-years-old. Being that he was only twenty-two, the idea of the eleven year age difference was both jarring and exciting.

"I know what you're thinking. I see you over there doing the math. You're trying to guess my age."

"No, it didn't even cross my mind," he lied.

"Most women in the industry are really funny about their ages. The way I see it, if you hide things like that, they'll probably come to light even faster. And with this Internet thing, it's probably just a matter of time before people start putting other people's business out there for the world to see. I doubt Ruby Dee or Bea Richards ever had to think about those kinds of things."

Troy nodded. "You mentioned Ruby Dee before. I take it you're a big fan of older actresses."

"I guess you could say that. In those older films, like *A Raisin in the Sun* and *Stormy Weather*, those women were classy and talented. Not to say that sisters aren't doing it well now, but it was just different back then, I guess. There was a lot more on the line." She paused. "Maybe I'm just romanticizing the past, but it just feels like those women were doing more than just acting. That's what I try to remind myself when I take a job: what I'm doing is bigger than just memorizing lines and saying them in front of a camera. The right role could change a life. I truly believe that."

Troy smiled awkwardly. "I guess I never really thought of it that way."

"When you finish film school, you'll probably make your own films. At first you'll probably be happy to be making films and getting paid to do it, but I imagine at some point you're going to give a lot of thought to what you want your art to say to people."

"Probably so," he responded. "So have you met any of the women you admire?"

Eris broke into a broad smile. "I actually met Ruby Dee once. It was at an NAACP banquet. I was too through! So much the fan that night! I even got my picture taken with her. I have it on my bedroom dresser. You know how you expect a person to be a certain way and it turns out that they are even more amazing than you originally thought? Well, that's Ruby Dee. I just love her to death!"

"Are you still in touch with her?"

"No. I only saw her that once—and to tell the truth, I'm not sure I would know what to say to her if I had to speak to her again. She leaves me completely speechless."

Troy smiled as he considered that someone as famous as Eris Perry could be that in awe of another actress. "That's really cool, your being a fan of someone like that. I didn't think famous people were fans of other famous people like that."

Her eyes still dancing from the memory of her encounter with Ruby Dee, Eris said, "We're all human beings, and human beings are always in awe of other human beings."

"Fair enough."

They sat staring at the glowing lights that illuminated the building in front of them, just beyond the overlook. Businesses lined the streets on either side, and the lights that illuminated everything around them were strong enough that he could have photographed the space around them as clearly as if it had been day.

Apropos of nothing, Troy said, "I haven't been able to stop thinking about you since you came by the brownstone on Sunday. This has all been so surreal. I'm still adjusting to being here with you."

Eris stretched out her arms and gazed up into the night sky. "I don't know why, but I feel like you're a really cool guy, and I guess that's why I asked you to come out with me again after what happened the other night. It's just hard for me, though. Some times I can't tell if a guy is really into me or if he's into who he thinks I am from the movies. That's the double edged sword of being well-known."

"I'm not gonna lie and say it never crossed my mind that you were Eris Perry, but being around you has shown me a very different side of you. I feel like I can tell you pretty much anything. When I got here this summer, I didn't know anybody, and then you came along and now I don't feel so—alone."

Eris placed her hand on his. "I know what you mean."

Troy lifted her hand to his lips and kissed it softly. She smiled in return.

"So," Eris said, "tell me about Ellison-Wright. Did you like it?"

Smiling, Troy told her about how Ellison-Wright was on the shortlist of colleges he had considered attending and how the deciding factor for him to go there was the fact that they had offered him a full academic scholarship—that and the mass communications program was among the best in the South. He talked about his freshman dorm and about later moving off-campus into a hotel downtown that had been converted into a co-ed dormitory. He talked about what it was like to pledge a fraternity during his junior year and even what it was like falling in and out of love in college.

"It all sounds amazing," Eris responded, once he had finished. "The closest I've come to college is playing a college student on television. But I keep wondering about what I missed out on when I came here."

"But if you had gone to school, you wouldn't be sitting here with me right now. I just believe that the decisions we make guide us to a singular result," he said.

"Something you learned in college?"

"Not really. Just something I believe about the way the world works. You had to bring that book by Aunt Flo's place at that exact time on that exact day for our paths to cross."

"So it's like fate or something?"

"In a way, yes."

His eyes met Eris's and they locked on each other, unflinching. For the first time since they met, he felt they were actually *seeing* each other, unguarded and honest.

"You're beautiful," he said.

She looked at him for a moment and then leaned in, kissing him deeply. He yielded to her touch, and in their cocoon of solitude, shielded from the stray tourists wandering down Sixth Avenue or down in the courtyard, Troy allowed his heart to rejoice in the moment.

Eris called Regina and had her arrange for a car to come and pick them up and take them back to Brooklyn. While they waited, Troy taught her how to play the "movie" game, something he and his classmates did for shits and giggles on Friday nights to blow off steam from the week's classes. The rules, as he explained them to her, were to not just say the lines from a movie, but to *deliver* them in the way the original actor had done. When the other person guessed the movie, then that person got to select and perform a new line. This was the first time Troy had ever played the game with a person who was actually in movies, though, so the game was that much more interesting.

Troy started the game off with a line from *The Color Purple*.

"Uh, you had her yo way—and I had her mine—but we both had her!"

"Danny Glover at the kitchen table with Shug's husband, right?"

"Yep," he said. "Your turn."

"My mama used to say ta me, 'Fleet—FLEET?— That's my name: Fleetwood Coupe de Ville. Mama had high ideals, y'know what I mean?'"

Troy doubled over laughing. "That's the lion from *The Wiz*. Okay, here's a hard one: 'I wanna hate you. I wake up every morning wanting to tell you to go to hell, but I don't. I guess you got a hold on me like that.'"

"Really?" Eris said, smiling. "Is that your best impression of me?"

"I can't do the lines justice like you did. That was so classic! I remember the first time I saw you in that scene with Denzel and how I thought to myself that he was the luckiest man on earth. He had a woman like you loving him."

"My character was supposed to be despicable—at least that's the way she was written in earlier drafts—but they changed the script a bit before production and made my character a little more complex. I'm glad for that. I doubt anyone would even remember that role if they hadn't."

"I went to see that movie three times, just to hear you say those words."

"Three times? Really? I think I've only seen the final version of the movie once. But I'm glad you enjoyed it."

He reached for her hand and felt her fingers interlock with his. "I know the car is on the way, but I wanted to ask you favor."

"What?" Eris said, looking a bit surprised.

"I want you to stay with me tonight," he said, then quickly added, "We don't have to sleep together. I just wanted enjoy your company until I fell asleep."

"Whoa, that's quite a request to lay on me. We've only been out twice, and to be honest, there's still a whole lot that I don't know about you. If we're gonna hang out, we need to take it real slow. I have to be careful because the level of trust I have to have before I go there with a man has to be strong enough to get over my fear that he would turn around and sell a story to *The Enquirer.*"

"What happened there? With *The Enquirer* thing?" Troy asked.

Eris sighed, as if she were unsure she wanted to go into the details. "I was dating this guy named Leighton," she finally said. "I met him at a record store in The Village. This was a little over three years ago. He played in this Afro-Punk band, and I just thought he was really something special. He said all the right things and did all the right things. We took in the city together. He wrote songs for me. I would even run my lines with him. That's how close we were. And although we'd only been together roughly a year, I was starting to see the possibilities of something more long term. I had even considered having him move into my place. When you love someone that much, you don't think anything of when they snap random pictures of you around the house while you're lounging in your underwear or getting out of the shower. I knew he did photography on the side, but I thought it was more like a jack-of-all-trades artist thing, kinda like when Miles Davis started painting. I wouldn't have thought in a million years that he would turn around and sell those pictures to a tabloid. I thank God that I wasn't actually naked in any of them!

"But it wasn't so much that they tried to concoct a story around his pictures as it was that he betrayed my trust. I would have done anything for that man, and to think he cared so little about my feelings—about me—that he'd go behind my back and do that to me hurt me more than anyone will ever know. The only person who really knows what I went through with Leighton is Flo. She was there helping me to get out of the funk I was in. I was so depressed and felt like I couldn't trust anyone, but Flo wouldn't give up on me.

"I remember one day she came over to my place and I was buried under a quilt on my couch, cartons of ice cream and all kinds of shit lying around the room, my curtains drawn tight, blocking out all of the light. She rang the doorbell for fifteen minutes, until I finally crawled out from under the quilt to answer the door. She came in and turned on the lights and started fixing up my place. She reminded me of what happened with Dante Wilbourne, how he had cheated on her with all of those rap video prostitutes, and told me that I had to pull my shit together, how I couldn't roll over and play dead just because some man did something to hurt me. She refused to give up on me.

"I think that's why we're as close as we are, because up until then, she was my friend, but after Leighton, she became my big sister, or the closest thing I ever had to one."

Troy didn't know what to say as he listened to her. He had been heartbroken while he was at Ellison-Wright, particularly when he was pledging his fraternity and his girlfriend at the time had dumped him, claiming it was impossible for them to fix their relationship when he was pledging and had so little time for her. All he had was his line brothers to help him through that time in his life, and his heart went out to Eris because she had had to deal with that type of situation, too.

"For whatever it's worth," he said, rubbing her hand, "I'd never hurt you like that. I've been through that experience, and I wouldn't wish it on anyone."

She squeezed his hand gently.

"What *do* you really want from me?" she asked, her voice quiet and serious.

"Just to enjoy your company. Yes, I'm seriously feeling you, but you're also the only real friend I have here—and I like that. I love hearing your voice, seeing your face, feeling the softness of your lips against mine. I know you have a life and all and that this is just another week in your life, but to me this is the illest moment in my life, bar none. I'm wide open like James Evans's nostrils."

She chuckled and then leaned over kissing Troy lightly. "Do me a favor. Don't assume what I'm thinking. You don't know if this is just another week in my life or not. If this was all just some trivial stuff, I would not be spending my time with you. I don't think either one of us has time to play games."

Troy nodded. "My bad. You're right."

The Town Car Regina called for earlier pulled up to the curb a few feet away from them. They hopped in.

"Where to?" the driver asked.

"Brooklyn Heights," Troy responded.

For the first few blocks, both he and Eris sat in silence.

"Is everything all right?" he finally asked quietly.

Eris looked at him and smiled. "Just thinking."

"Thinking about what?"

"About whether or not I'm gonna go home with you."

Troy was unable to conceal the huge smile growing across his face. "What can I do to help you make up your mind?"

"I don't know. I guess it's just a matter of trusting you."

"Well, what can I do to make you trust me?" he said.

"I just need some time to think."

As the car drove onto the Brooklyn Bridge, Troy could see the abyss of darkness resting between the two boroughs. The East River was out there somewhere, beside and beneath them, and soon they would be on the other side of the bridge, in Brooklyn, minutes from the brownstone. Eris still had not said anything to him or the driver about her intentions.

The car seemed to move quickly through the Brooklyn Heights neighborhood, and Troy silently wished the driver would slow down to a creep—just until he knew what Eris had planned to do.

The Town Car pulled up in front of the brownstone, and Troy opened his door, which was facing the curb. Once he stood up, he noticed that Eris had not moved.

He extended his hand to her. "Please come with me."

She looked at his hand for a moment, the car idling in the darkness of the street. "Don't make me regret this," she said, taking his hand.

Once they walked up the steps of the brownstone, Troy looked back. The car was already gone, and Eris had chosen him.

Eris took a seat on Troy's bed and kicked off her heels, while he stood in the corner hanging up his blazer.

"I need to hop in the shower. I sweated my ass off earlier, and I don't want to have you talking about how funky I am," he said.

Eris chuckled, while looking around the room and taking in Aunt Flo's interior decorating.

When he saw that she was caught up in the layout of the bedroom, the Ernie Barnes prints on the walls and the various African American collectibles situated around the room, he added, "You're welcome to join me." He meant it in jest, but when he saw the surprised expression on her face, he backpedaled. "I'm just joking."

"Whatever. You know that was a real invitation," she responded, needling him.

"I was just saying something."

"Well, I think I'll be just fine. You can do this one by yourself," she said playfully.

"I'll be back in a few minutes. Just make yourself comfortable."

Troy left Eris stretched across the bed, thumbing through the copy of *Mama Day* he had brought up earlier from the library, while he walked down the hall to hop in the shower.

As he stood beneath the blast of water from the shower head, he wondered what Eris was doing while he cleaned himself. She had agreed to stay with him for the night, so he tried to interpret exactly what that meant to her. In college if a woman slept over at his apartment, that meant something was definitely going down on the sex tip. Just from Eris's mannerisms he knew that she viewed the situation a bit differently. She would kiss him and do things to show she liked him, but there was clearly a line that she was choosing not to cross at this point. As he pondered this, he realized that she was much more than someone to whom he was physically attracted; she was a friend. He loved talking to her, and he realized that was hardly a poor consolation should she not kiss him again that evening.

Once he finished showering, he tossed on the mesh basketball shorts he used as pajamas and a loose fitting t-shirt. There was nothing impressive about what he slept in, but he doubted he needed to be impressive given the fact that he would not be seducing her then. If she had decided to join him in the shower, that would have been another story. But she hadn't.

Troy entered the bedroom to find Eris stretched across the bed in one of his extra-large t-shirts and little else. The book was open in front of her as she lay on her stomach facing the direction of the pillows. From this angle, he could see the smoothness of the backs of her shapely legs extending from beneath the t-shirt and the rise of her ass like a gorgeous Georgia hill stretching the cotton fabric above it. The visual of her lying there in his clothing was beyond arousing, and he found himself stiffening under the mesh of his basketball shorts.

"Hey," he said. "I'm really feeling your change of clothes."

"Well, I needed something to sleep in, so I hope you don't mind that I grabbed one of your t-shirts out the dresser."

"Not at all. I'm not gonna lie, though. You look sexy as hell in that shirt."

Eris smiled, rolling over and scooting to the edge of the bed closest to him. "So you have me here. Now what?"

"You mean it's really that simple?"

"What do you mean?" she asked.

"Just tell you what I want to do?"

"Surprise me," she said.

"Well—" he started.

"Just don't say what I think you're gonna say. Be more original than that."

"But how do you know what I'm gonna say?"

"You're a guy."

"That's cold—and it's a stereotype on top of that," Troy said, laughing.

"So you weren't gonna say that you wanted to have sex with me?"

"Huh?" he responded, blushing. "What do you mean?"

"You heard me."

"Why? Would that have been so wrong, I mean given the circumstances?"

Eris stood up and approached him, pointing a finger softly into his chest. "*You* told me that you wanted to fall asleep talking to me. That's all you said. So, Troy, you should probably get to talking."

Her mannerisms were entirely coy, and he sensed she was a few seconds away from flat-out seducing him. Still, he marveled at her control of the environment. Everything was completely subject to her authority, and he loved every moment of it.

"I'm glad you're here," he said. "I guess I should start with that."

"Okay."

"And I had a wonderful evening."

"So far?"

"So far," he repeated. "And I can't stop thinking about kissing you."

He lifted her chin so that their lips met, and he savored the smooth, free movements of her tongue against his. He could feel her fingernails gently caressing the back of his neck and the warmth of her body pressing itself steadily against his.

She lifted her head, allowing him full access to her neck, and as he traced his kisses along her nape, he could feel her breath in soft, staccato exhalations, tickling his skin.

"Troy," she whispered. "As much as I like this, I just have to tell you one thing. I don't want to have sex with you tonight. Is that going to be a problem?"

With the persistent throbbing of his erection, pressed against her stomach through the fabric of her t-shirt and his basketball shorts, he felt the sting of disappointment. "It's cool," he allowed himself to say, before adding, "but why?"

"Try to see it from my perspective. I just met you, and I like you. But I don't want to move too fast with this. And you'll be gone in a few weeks anyway. I'm not into one night stands or selling myself short just because I'm attracted to a guy."

"I'm only going to L.A. That's like a second home to you, right? Hollywood and all."

"It doesn't work like that. I shoot in various locations, and when I'm working, I'm working. When I'm not, I live here in Brooklyn. My work and private lives are separate. I told you that when we first met."

Troy could feel the conversation pushing both of them out of the moment. There would be plenty of time to talk about their future together and how they would be able to continue building something, despite the distance. Right now, however, he could only focus on the feel of her body's warmth against him. He quickly kissed her again and sighed with relief when she placed her hand on his chest and caressed it.

"Hold on," Troy said, reaching over and dimming the lights in the room for atmospheric effect.

They found their way onto the bed and lay side by side, kissing each other. She eased off his shirt and he took off hers, and within moments the only things separating their bodies were their underwear. Troy reached for her panties and begin to pull them down, when she stopped him.

"I told you that I can't do that."

"We don't have to do that," he responded.

"Nothing good would come of us being completely naked in this bed. Trust me."

"I want you so badly right now. Are you telling me that you don't want me right here, right now?"

"It's not about what my body wants at this moment. It's about what my heart and mind will be able to live with in the morning," Eris said.

"I understand," Troy said, although being so close to her like this was killing him. "Wait. I have an idea."

"What?"

"Take off your panties."

"Troy, come on."

"Seriously. I won't touch you. Trust me. I'll do the same."

"Well, now I know I won't be doing that then," she responded.

"Please. Just trust me."

"First, tell me what you you have planned."

Troy sat up in the bed, resting on his elbows and looked into Eris's face. He could barely make it out from the thin veil of light that slid through the wooden blinds over the window and the dull glow coming from the nearby lamp.

"We'll lie down back-to-back, completely naked. But we won't touch. You will know that I'm not wearing anything, and I will know that you're not wearing anything either. We'll be close enough to feel the body heat of the other, but not close enough to actually be touching."

"And?"

"And then you will touch yourself, and I will touch myself, and then we can hear each other breathing and fantasize about being with the other person, and you can hear my voice, and I can hear your voice."

Eris started to chuckle softly. "How in the world did you come up with that idea?"

"It was the only thing I could think of that would allow us to be together without *being* together, if you know what I mean."

"That's just going to make me want you more," she said.

"Maybe, but at least you can have a release without the guilt of actually having sex."

He could see her shaking her head in disbelief. "That sounds so crazy."

"Hey it's just a thought, and I can't even say it's the best thought. But at least it's something," he said.

Eris was silent as she considered this. Her body body was so still she resembled a statue. Inside, Troy ached with anticipation.

"Okay. Turn your back," she finally said.

He quickly and nervously complied.

"I'm taking off my panties now."

Troy could feel her body shifting in the bed behind him and feel the covers move as she lifted her hand and placed her underwear on the dresser.

"Your turn," she said.

Troy quickly slid out of his underwear and lay anxiously facing the wall, the faintest bit of her body heat inches from his skin. "How do I know you're really naked," he said.

Eris grabbed his hand and placed it on her bare hip. Once he felt the warmth and smoothness of her skin, he took her hand and placed it on his hip.

"Okay. No more touching from this point forward," Eris said.

"Sure," Troy said, feeling the overwhelming nervousness of the moment.

They began slowly and in silence, their hands moving in cautious, deliberate rhythms, the thin sheet of the bed rising and falling with each movement, their voices punctuating the space with occasional moans of self-gratification.

Then Eris spoke.

"Troy, tell me what you're doing to me right now," she said, her voice a raspy whisper. It was the voice of a person who had been on the phone for hours with a lover and was approaching the climax of conversational intimacy.

Troy was suddenly pulled from his thoughts and was now being welcomed into Eris's fantasy. While the idea of what she was doing excited him even more, he worried that he might say the wrong thing and kill her flow. He offered, "I'm planting kisses along your stomach and onto your hips. Can you feel my tongue, moist against your inner thighs?" He knew he was struggling. He would have rather spoken with his actions than his words, but she was leaving him little choice in the matter.

"How do I taste?" she said between moans.

"Incredible," he responded. "You are all that I want."

And then they fell silent again, and their voices were replaced with Eris's legs working furiously against the bed, struggling to gain traction on the damp sheets. Troy could only imagine what she looked like enveloped in the ecstasy of orgasm. He found himself so fascinated with his thoughts of her movements that he stopped touching himself and focused all of his attention on the violent shudder of her body and the crescendoing moan that rose in her throat, a primal melody, and filled the room like a tropical rain cloud bursting and releasing its storm down on the myriad of trees below.

When she climaxed, she backed up into him, her naked body moist with perspiration sliding wickedly against his. The touch of her warm, wet skin was electric, and Troy could not resist the urge to touch himself again and lose himself in the moment, climaxing shortly afterwards.

They lay side by side, the silence of the room attacked by the percussion of their breathing.

"Damn, I'm gonna need another shower again," he said jokingly.

Eris chuckled, running her hand across her flat stomach, the definition of her abs appearing with the exhalation of each breath. "I know I definitely need one at this point."

"So will you join me *now*?" Troy asked. He figured it was worth another try, although he kept his expectations modest.

"As long as you remember our arrangement," she responded, sitting up in the bed and brushing her hair from her damp cheeks.

Smiling, and quietly brimming with confidence, Troy walked down the hall and started up the shower again. This time Eris would be joining him.

They took their time bathing each other, and Troy absorbed each of her body parts with his eyes and hands, memorizing every centimeter of her skin, the ease of her smile, the curve of her body, the way her hair hugged her face in the moisture of the bathroom, that dimpled smile, those phenomenal legs, even the delicateness of her hands and feet, all for posterity. But her eyes were what really took away his ability to think clearly. Her eyes were wide, beautiful, playful, and mysterious, all in one. They were so animated she could simply communicate all of her thoughts without once moving her lips. Those were the eyes that had made her a movie star, and those were the eyes that had peeked into his soul and taken a piece of who he was with them. Yes, it was that look she gave him that scared him the most; it was a look that made him want to love her even when he knew the improbability of her loving him back.

After carefully drying each other, they returned to his bedroom and, still naked, lay down and snuggled in the bed, cloaked only in a blanket of darkness.

"Are you still awake?" Eris asked twenty minutes later.

"I couldn't sleep if I tried."

"Me neither," she said. Still facing the wall, she asked, "What was it like where you grew up?"

Troy thought it a strange question to ask someone you were lying in bed naked with, but he didn't mind. He would have answered any question that she asked, simply because he enjoyed the beauty of her soft, raspiness voice. It was a bedroom voice, one that he had the unique pleasure of experiencing directly.

"I grew up in Gloucester, not too far from Williamsburg and Yorktown. It's in the eastern part of the state, just off the water. I'd have to say that it was nice. A lot of history in the area. Also, there's a lot of natural beauty with the beaches and trees and trails. My mother is a librarian, so I spent a lot of time there, reading books and stuff. My dad is an optometrist with an office in Newport News. Neither one of them is from the area, but they had moved there a year before I was born and had decided to stay, so that's where I ended up growing up. What about you? What was it like in Louisiana?"

"I enjoyed Monroe. Relatively speaking, we have a pretty good parish, and we don't have some of the problems of larger cities like Shreveport and New Orleans. On the other hand, we don't have the same kind of entertainment, either. Shreveport and New Orleans have the casinos, the tourists, the sporting events, and the money. Monroe is just a plucky place where people handle their business and try to do the best they can. I think it's a great place to grow up, but for what I wanted to do with my life, Monroe couldn't do it for me," Eris said.

"Maybe one day you could show me around there," Troy said.

Eris let the comment fall flat and waited a beat before speaking again. "I have a question for you. What is it that you see happening between us?"

"I don't know. I would definitely like to date you with an eye towards something serious and exclusive. I'm really into you, and I'm open to all of the possibilities."

Eris laid her head upon Troy's chest. "I need to ask you something."

"Shoot."

"My age is not going to be a problem for you, is it? I mean, I know you said you were cool, but once the novelty of the newness of things wears off, will you still feel the same way?"

"I guarantee that it won't be an issue. You don't get it. You're my dream girl. I have fantasized about you for quite a while, and being here with you like this is beyond anything I could have ever imagined," he said.

Eris didn't respond, only nuzzling her head against his chest.

They lay in silence while the sound of the occasional car passing through the night streets or the soft breeze tip-toeing off the East River found its way against the window sill. Pretty soon Troy could hear the deep breaths of Eris's sleep, and he closed his eyes, capping off one of the most amazing nights of his life.

Troy awoke the following morning from the sound of Eris moving around the bedroom.

"Good morning," he said, barely opening his eyes. "You wanna get some breakfast? There's a great diner about a block away. Pancakes like you wouldn't believe!"

"No, that's all right," Eris responded, sitting in a chair across the room, facing the bed. She was putting on her stiletto heels and had already dressed in her clothes from the previous night.

"Are you leaving?"

"I need to get home."

"Are you coming back? I was kinda hoping maybe we could spend the day together or something like that."

Eris finished putting on her shoes and looked up. Her eyes met Troy's and she held that gaze for a moment before shaking her head. "I'm not coming back."

"Plans for the day already? Well, what about tomorrow?"

"Troy, I'm not coming back to see you at all while you're here."

Troy jumped up from the bed and walked over to her, taking her hands in his. "Why? Did I do something wrong? I thought we had a good time last night."

"It *was* nice, but I can't do this."

"Do what?"

"*This*," she said, waiving a hand around the room. "The truth is that I shouldn't have stayed over last night. And I probably shouldn't have done any of the things I did with you before. That was careless of me. I had my guard down."

Troy took a seat on the ottoman near the chair. "I'm so confused right now. Where is all of this coming from? Do you have someone special in your life already?"

"It's not even about that. I'd rather we just cut our losses here."

Troy reached for his clothes and started dressing while Eris grabbed her tote bag. He followed her out of the bedroom and into the den.

"Just tell me what I did wrong, so I can fix it," he said, following her across the room.

She stopped and turned to face him. "You said something last night that made me realize that this wouldn't work no matter what we did."

Troy reached for her hand and guided her to the sofa. "Let's sit down and talk. Even if you decide to leave, we can at least know that we understand what the other is thinking. Can we at least do that?"

She nodded and took a seat next to him.

"Okay. What did I say that rubbed you the wrong way?"

Eris looked away, either embarrassed or distraught by what she was going to say. Troy could not tell how to interpret any of her actions at this point. "You called me your dream girl."

Troy was incredulous. How in the world was that a bad thing? Most women would have been flattered to high heaven and back if a man said those words to them. In that moment, he realized that he just didn't understand Eris, who was proving to be atypical of everything he had ever experienced with a woman during his lifetime. He took a deep breath and said as calmly as he could muster, "Eris, could you please tell me how what I said was a bad thing?"

"It's not just that time, but you've said things throughout the entire time we've been hanging out that make me feel like you're not really interested in *me*, but in who you think I am. You have me on this pedestal in your mind, like I'm some kind of queen. If I weren't famous, I doubt you'd even be interested. I definitely wouldn't be your *dream girl*."

Was she serious? Troy felt blindsided by what he figured was a mountain of insecurity on her part. "I didn't mean that you were my dream girl because I knew who you were before we met. I'm so past the fact that you're famous."

"Are you really?"

"Yes."

"Then why don't I believe you?"

Troy sighed. "I can't tell you what to believe or not believe. All I can tell you is that I have been 100 percent genuine with you from the first moment we met. And wasn't it you who told me to not assume I knew what you were thinking earlier? At least give me some credit that you don't really know what I'm thinking either. You don't know if I'd be interested in you or not. I get that. But if I tell you that I'm interested in you and that my reasons for being interested in you are because of the way you make me feel, I don't think you should ignore that just because you're worried about experiencing something new."

Eris grabbed her bag and stood. "I have to be able to trust your intentions, and right now, whether they are true or not, I can't tell. And since I can't tell, I have no choice but to protect myself."

"Protect yourself from me? Eris, I would never, I mean *never*, do anything to hurt you. But I'm starting to think that it doesn't matter what I tell you anymore. Just look at my actions. I have not taken advantage of your trust. I have not even told anyone about our spending time together. But you already know all of this. So what's really the deal?"

"It's just hard for me," she finally admitted through an exasperated sigh. It was as if she blamed herself just as much as she did her partner. "The last time I dated someone who wasn't in the industry, he tried to take pictures of me and sell them to a tabloid. The entire situation was embarrassing and hurtful. I felt like such a fool for thinking he and I had something special."

Troy placed a hand on Eris's shoulder. "I'm not him. That's all I can say. I would never do that to you. That's not who I am."

"I'm not trying to take this all out on you, but I need some space right now. I've already called for a car, and it should be here in a minute."

He shrugged his shoulders. "At least let me sit with you while you wait."

"Okay," she said softly.

They both sat back on the sofa, and Eris turned her attention to the rest of the room, looking at the art and photography on the walls, avoiding eye contact with Troy.

He sat back on the sofa with his head lifted to the ceiling, trying to not let the situation frustrate him while she sat so closely.

"The first time I heard 'Big Poppa' was at a step show the year before I pledged. I was like 'Who is this dude?' His voice was heavy and lispy. I remember a journalist saying that it sounded like a 'wet explosion.' But in spite of that, his flow was original and smart, you know? It was refreshing how smoothly he told stories."

Eris turned her attention back towards him, so he continued, "Back when Tupac died, I didn't believe it for two seconds. He had been shot before and survived. I figured he couldn't be killed—at least not with bullets. He died on Friday the 13th, too. It was one of those evenings that felt strange. I couldn't stop thinking about him for weeks. Then in March, Biggie. It all felt so strange. How did two of the best emcees in the game wind up dead? Hip-hop used to be fun. I remember doing the prep to L.L. Cool J's 'Around the Way Girl' and now I was seeing my favorite emcees get buried.

"I don't even know why I'm telling you any of this. I just know when Aunt Flo asked me if I wanted to housesit for her, I didn't hesitate to accept her offer. After all, this is Brooklyn. Maybe not Brooklyn like Bed Stuy, but it's still the borough. It just felt like the place I was supposed to be. And then you came along, and it was beautiful.

"And now you're leaving, and I guess it shouldn't matter, since I'll be heading back to Gloucester before the end of the month, but it does. It cuts me deep that you think you can't take me at my word. And I realize there's nothing I can do to convince you otherwise at this point. If this winds up being the last time we talk, I just want you to know that you have given me one of the most wonderful times of my life. The whole situation is the illest, though. I always found certain words to be funny because they mean opposites, like sanction and sanction, and the word 'ill' is like that. It's good and bad, and when I used that word with you earlier, it was all good. Now, it feels like it could go either way, because I'm happy for the time we're spending, but I'm sad that you feel you can't trust me about my feelings for you."

Just then Eris's cell phone rang, and she quickly answered. Once she hung up, she said, "The car is downstairs. I have to go."

Troy nodded. "So you don't have any response to anything that I've said?"

"What do you want me to say?"

"Say that you'll give me a chance."

Eris walked down the stairs and Troy followed her. As she reached for the front door, Troy grabbed her hand and stopped her, pulling her body to his, and kissing her deeply. She allowed him to enter her mouth, and she quickly reciprocated. Then almost as quickly as it had begun, it ended.

"You were always a good kisser," she said, opening the door and walking across the sidewalk to the car. Troy stood in the doorway watching her.

He waived to her as the car pulled away from the curb, but due to the tint on the windows, he couldn't see if she returned his wave or not.

He wanted to believe that she had seen him, but he was no more convinced of that than she had claimed to be of his feelings toward her.

She would figure out he was telling the truth, he knew. He just hoped that she did so before he was gone.

In the days that followed, Troy found himself staying close to home, in hopes that Eris would call or perhaps stop by the brownstone. But with each day silent, no different from the last, it dawned on him that maybe this *was* the end. Maybe the arc of their story had climaxed around the same time their bodies had. The slow days leading toward Aunt Flo's return were the denouement, unsatisfactory as it was.

He used her phone number once during the second day after her departure and left a message, where he reiterated some of the same points that he had the last time she was there. He never received a call back.

He had also spent a few hours out of each day wandering the promenade, hoping to cross paths with her.

Their ending had come too abruptly, and he was ill-prepared to spend his last days in Brooklyn alone and was astonished that he'd allowed himself to be there for nearly a month and only make one friend the entire time. He knew that he was not the most sociable of people, but this was totally unlike him to not meet *anyone* outside of Eris Perry.

His loneliness gave way to fatigue, and during the day before Aunt Flo was to return (and he was to leave), he packed up all of his things, choosing to spend the final twenty-four hours of his Brooklyn Heights adventure living directly from his suitcase.

For lunch, he walked across the way to Fulton Street, where the cacophonic blend of music and street activity was the antithesis of the quiet, peaceful streets of Brooklyn Heights. The shopping area reminded him of 125th Street in Harlem. Posters and t-shirts of Biggie hung in windows, vendors spread out bootleg movies on blankets in front of stores, and every manner of oil-based fragrance, handmade jewelry, and artwork could be found along the sidewalks. He had only been to this neighborhood a few times, but he knew he wanted to at least come back one more time—maybe just to say goodbye. He grabbed a sandwich from one of the bodegas lining Fulton, bought a t-shirt of Biggie standing on a corner in Bed Stuy throwing dice, and headed back toward Brooklyn Heights.

He had already given up checking for Eris in the ocean of black people filling the neighborhood. Instead, he observed every conceivable shade of brown, a tableau of the uniqueness of a people, moving about. If Eris were out there somewhere, Troy chose not to separate her from the milieu of Afrocentricity that lay before him.

By the time he made it onto Montague, he had already begun to visualize what was coming in the next few weeks. He would only be home in Gloucester for a few weeks before he flew out to California to begin the next phase of his life.

The idea of being a student filmmaker in Los Angeles was intimidating on a number of levels. All of the major movie studios were within half an hour of the school, and he had heard that it was not uncommon for directors and producers to drop by the schools (some of them their alma maters) to see what was new—or better yet, who was the new talented kid on the block. And with it being 1997, the word on the street was that black directors were on the rise. The industry had clearly come a long way from the days of Oscar Micheaux.

When Troy had first taken an interest in film, it had been because of Spike Lee's *School Daze*. It had started there, but he would eventually go back and watch all of the films made by Melvin Van Peebles and Gordon Parks, too. There was even a kid named Matty Rich who had made some noise in New York with *Straight Out of Brooklyn*. John Singleton, however, was the reigning black director on the block when Troy made it to

Ellison-Wright. *Boyz in the Hood* had been a classic that, for better or worse, inspired a number of other films with darker urban themes, like the Hughes brothers' ultra-violent gangster movie, *Menace II Society.*

Troy had not yet decided what types of films he wanted to make, only that he wanted to make them. Having grown up on a steady diet of Stephen King and Edgar Allan Poe, he was leaning towards more macabre content, but he was open for the moment. He couldn't point his finger to any famous black directors who had done horror movies, other than Rusty Cundieff with his movie *Tales From the Hood*, a film that bordered on being comedy just as much as it was billed as horror. The absence of any other known black directors in the genre was more of an invitation than a turn off, as far as Troy was concerned. He would just need to make the film that would open doors for other young black directors.

His mind was still racing with thoughts of his filmmaking future when he arrived at the brownstone. He half-expected to see another note attached to the front door, one where Eris apologized for what happened and offered to make amends during his last evening. That idea didn't make much sense, though. She had gone more than a week and a half without contacting him, and he was unclear of when she was leaving for Vancouver to shoot her new film. It was like he was never a part of her world. The three times he had been with her seemed like moments where their worlds had just happened to collide—with a fury—and afterwards it was like the moments never even happened.

Troy hated the idea that he could share an intimate moment with a woman he truly liked only to have her disappear into thin air the next day. If this were a movie, he figured, there would have been some kind of happy ending. For example, there would have been a note on the door, or as he walked into the brownstone, there would have been something there waiting for him, an apology of sorts—or even a chance for him to apologize (for what, he was unsure). Or maybe there would have been a voicemail for him (of course there wasn't). Yeah, if this was a movie, he figured, that audience would have walked out of the movie pissed off that real life had trumped the fantasy of predictability.

He walked upstairs to his bedroom and marveled at how clean the space was. When he had arrived, it looked like an unused guest room. He had quickly transformed it into a lived-in room, one that bore more of his particular style. Now the room had gone full circle, and it looked as it had when he first arrived. He had already washed all of the dishes and cleaned up the sections of the room that he had frequented. He wanted Aunt Flo to return to an immaculate place, and once he removed his suitcase and backpack, it would be as if he had never been there.

He would miss the brownstone, true, but he was also ready to leave. He missed Gloucester and his parents, and the friends he had grown up with. He needed that time to be loved and doted on before he left for his new home on the West Coast.

He was so absorbed in his thoughts, that he almost missed the ringing of the phone. He picked up the cordless on the dresser in his room.

"Hello?"

"Hello, is this Troy?"

"Yes."

"This is Regina, Eris's assistant. I've been trying to call you for a few days now, but I accidentally mixed up the last two numbers in your phone number. I just realized it this afternoon, and I wanted to reach out to you and pass along a message from Eris."

Troy thought to himself, "Not this shit again." Regina had to have been the most incompetent personal assistant in the entire industry who still had a job. Getting the delayed message was akin to standing outside in the heat, sweating through his dress shirt, waiting outside a club where the bouncer took pleasure in his discomfort.

"Hi, Regina. What's the message?" His voice was flat and pained. He felt like he was on the verge of getting on the merry-go-round again: Eris charms him and makes him feel incredible; she then abandons him and then comes back to pick him up off the ground, but she has trouble contacting him before finally finding him; and the cycle repeats.

"She wanted me to tell you that she's on location in Vancouver right now but she will be in L.A. in October. I believe she said you'd be at USC this fall. Anyway, she wanted to see if you'd be interested in getting together for dinner."

Troy laughed.

"I'm sorry," Regina said. "Did I say something funny?"

"No, I'm just trippin' that she can book a dinner months in advance."

"That's just Hollywood," Regina said. "You plan out as far as you can."

"I see."

"She has an opening on October 17th at six o'clock. Should I pencil you in?"

Pencil me in, Troy thought. So this was how it was going to be with Eris? That did not sit well with him. He wasn't Eddie Murphy, she wasn't Robin Givens, and this wasn't *Boomerang*.

Still, he couldn't deny there was still a big part of him that longed to see her, if only for a moment. Maybe he could build with her that trust she so desperately needed with him to move forward. Clearly, she wanted the same thing as he, or she wouldn't have bothered reaching out to him.

He thought about lying in bed, back-to-back with her, hearing her moans creeping up his back into a thunderous, orgasmic punctuation. He thought about standing beneath the hot spray of the shower, washing her, his hands caressing her naked skin. He also thought about the feeling of her head lying on his chest, her soft breaths tickling him. There was definitely something there. She didn't have to take him to dinner or take him to the fashion show or even spend the night with him, but she had done all of those things. She was just trying to get herself into a space to feel better about what they were doing.

Maybe that was it.

Or maybe this was a game to her. She knew she could treat him any type of way and get away with it, because he was totally into her. She knew how to turn on her charm and how to manipulate him, if she needed to. There was not a single thing that had happened since Troy met her that was not in some way controlled by Eris. In many ways, he felt like an enthusiastic puppet.

He was torn, his ambivalence clouding his thoughts, as his fingers adjusted themselves around the phone.

Was there a future with Eris Perry, or did only confusion and heartache lie ahead?

Troy glanced around his bedroom, seeking traces of Eris within the space.

She had been there, right?

It was now difficult to tell. He closed his eyes trying to remember the taste of her kisses, the kisses that she claimed to have liked as much as he.

"Troy, are you still there?" he could hear Regina say. Her voice was not brazenly abrasive, but beneath its smooth, somewhat smug, timbre was the scraping quality that served as a reminder of this ever so slight hierarchical stratifyer. Her boss was famous; he, however, was not.

"Yeah, sorry about that. The phone connection was a little weak where I was standing."

"Oh, okay. Well, is the 17ᵗʰ of October good for you?"

So this was what it all boiled down to, he thought, as he slowly paced back and forth across the hard wood floor of the room. This was the solitary thing that stood between him and Eris.

Seemingly simple. A one-word answer, at best.

He held the receiver close to his mouth, his lips parting, aching desperately not to betray his sense of self. He deserved a respect Eris had not entirely shown him, and he thought briefly about holding out, forcing her to be more respectful of his time and feelings, to stop playing games, and to even give him the benefit of the doubt that he would not be the asshole that her last boyfriend was. Surely he could demand at least these few things of her before he committed any more of himself to this situation, but who was he kidding? This was Eris Perry.

Maybe she had been right when she said that he would be unable to see her as anything other than famous—well, maybe not in those exact words—and he had wanted to reject that idea a hundred times over, but with Eris's assistant on the phone scheduling a date months in advance, he could not help but be reminded of this basic, incontrovertible fact.

He knew before he heard the sound of his voice, nearly bass-less from mild disuse and almost a muddled tinny whisper, that his response to Regina's question would be simple, plain, and unadulterated: "Yes."

Special Thanks

Thank you to Sabin Prentis, Torrey H. Walker, Van G. Garrett, Nsayel Mputubwele, Shonda Buchanan, Randolph and Jean Walker, Joi and DeWayne Whittington, Phill Branch, Jay Craft, Daniel Black, Erica "RivaFlowz" Buddington, Mat Johnson, Victor LaValle, Richard Wall, Philippe Loubat-Delranc, my French publishing family at Édition Autrement, and all of my friends, students, and fellow writers who have offered support for this project in its various shapes over the years.

But above all, I want to thank my wife, Lauren, and my daughter, Zoë, for their undying support, encouragement, and love. Without them, this book would not have been possible.

AUTHOR BIO

Ran Walker is a native Mississippian who gave up the practice of law to become a writer. He is also the author of five novels. His work has appeared in various anthologies and literary journals, and he was awarded several fellowships, including the Mississippi Arts Commission/National Endowment for the Arts Fellowship for Creative Nonfiction in 2005. He has participated in both the Hurston-Wright Writers Workshop and the Callaloo Writers Workshop.

Walker serves as a creative writing professor at Hampton University and enjoys spending his time reading, composing music, taking photographs with his iPhone, and exploring the country with his wife, Lauren, and daughter, Zoë.

He can be reached at www.ranwalker.com.

Proof

Made in the USA
Charleston, SC
08 November 2015